Bear Me in Mind

A Novel

Dawn Chalker

Hepatica Books

Cover design by Briana Chalker
Cover photo by Dawn Chalker
Author photo by Briana Chalker

Library of Congress Control Number: 2022915430

ISBN 979-8-218-05509-7

Hepatica Books
Traverse City, Michigan
hepaticabooks.com

To Briana and Peter

Those who contemplate the beauty of the earth find reserves
of strength that will endure as long as life lasts.
— Rachel Carson,
Silent Spring

Chapter 1

Wednesday

Taking a picture of a tourist couple at their request seemed like a harmless thing to do. Little did Emily know what events would be set in motion.

Emily stood on the wooden platform built on the cliff that overlooked Lake Michigan on a mild day in May. Gentle waves rolled in on the long, sandy beach below. Sun poured down as warm as honey, and a soft breeze caressed her face. During a cool, windy April, she had felt spring would never come this year.

The lake stretched to the horizon. A pair of islands rose up in the distance. With no mist to obscure them, she could pick out details on the islands. Looking down over the railing, she watched an eagle soar slowly across the tree tops.

A few feet away from her, a young couple stood close together at the railing, gesturing at the view. They were dressed in khakis and hooded sweatshirts, one red and one white, with the park logo on the front. The young man pointed at the islands and exclaimed at the vastness of the lake, how they couldn't see the shore on the other side. The young woman smiled at him and agreed that the Lake was much larger than they had thought it would be.

Emily smiled to herself. Lake Michigan often surprised people who had never seen the Great Lakes. Five large lakes formed by a glacier long ago. From shore, one could look as far as the eye could see and not see the other side. The unsalted ocean, some locals called them. And the views from the Cliffs Trail were always spectacular, whatever the weather.

The young man turned toward Emily. "Do you know the names of those two islands? They look quite large from here."

Surprised, Emily turned from gazing at the water to look at the young couple. She guessed they were in their twenties.

The young man smiled at her and pointed to the two islands in the distance, straight out from shore.

"North and South Manitou. The islands are named after a legend."

"What kind of a legend?" The woman looked at Emily intently.

"It's an Anishinaabe legend about how a mother bear and her two cubs crossed Lake Michigan, fleeing a fire in Wisconsin. The two bear cubs didn't make it to the mainland and were turned into islands, some say by their mother, some say by the Great Spirit. The mother bear became a sand dune to watch over her cubs." Emily pointed toward the large dune on the left. "That's the mother bear."

"Sounds a bit grim." The young woman frowned.

"A bit sad, I suppose. The Anishinaabe lived in this area for centuries and still live here. The islands are important to them. The dune of the mother bear is a sacred landmark and represents the mother's love and sorrow for her cubs."

"Does anyone live on the islands? Do people go there?"

"No one lives on the islands year around, but South Manitou has a museum, a campground, and some other sights. There's a ferry that makes a round trip once a day, so if you go you have to stay all day until the ferry returns. North Manitou has a cemetery that is important to the Indigenous people. Camping and backpacking are allowed. Some research people stay on the island in the summer to count the piping plovers."

"Interesting." The young man nodded. "I'd like to go there."

"What are piping plovers? They sound like they should play an instrument." The young woman furrowed her forehead.

"Shorebirds that were becoming extinct until recently. Now people are trying to protect their nesting areas. Researchers count how many plovers are born each year to see if the birds are recovering."

"That seems like a good idea. Are they recovering?"

"I think they had a good year. More new chicks were counted."

"Sorry. I have to check my phone." Emily pulled out her phone and checked the time. She needed to be at work by noon today, to get ready for a group of high school students who were coming to the Nature Center for a presentation and hike. The handouts were ready, but she wanted to get the room set up and review what she would say.

She put her phone back in her pocket and smiled at the couple. "It was nice meeting you. Enjoy your hike."

"Nice meeting you, too, and thanks for telling us about the islands." The couple smiled again and turned back to look at the lake.

Emily walked down the short, dirt path that led to the main trail. As she hiked down the hill, she admired the wildflowers that grew on either side of the trail. She didn't need to photograph the trout lilies and spring beauties. She had photographed them before, But she enjoyed their early arrival, signaling the beginning of wildflower season.

Farther down the trail, she spotted some flowers she had not yet photographed. When she had seen them in the wildflower book, the name intrigued her, fringed polygala. These were the first ones she had seen this spring. She took out her camera and knelt down to get a close-up picture, one that would highlight the fringed tongue-like purple petals that gave the flower its name.

Voices from higher up the hill alerted her that people were hiking down the trail toward her. As she stood up to let them pass, the couple she had talked to on the platform stopped beside her. She nodded to acknowledge that she remembered them.

The young man gave her a big smile. He gestured to the camera. "You are a photographer. Would you please take our picture?"

"Of course." Emily often had her camera with her and was asked by tourists to take their pictures. Usually, they just wanted a photo on a phone camera, which didn't really require a photographer.

The young woman smiled shyly and handed Emily her phone. "We are on our honeymoon. We have never seen Lake Michigan or any of the Great Lakes before. They are much bigger than we imagined."

Emily took the phone. "The Great Lakes are always impressive. Congratulations on your honeymoon. Where are you from?"

"We're from Kansas. Friends of ours told us it is beautiful up here in the spring, and we have wanted to see the Great Lakes for a while."

"I guess there aren't many lakes in Kansas?" Emily had once driven through Kansas with a friend during a hot July day. With no trees in sight. Kansas had seemed very dry. She had thought then that she would not want to live where there were no big lakes like Lake Michigan and the other Great Lakes. That was probably one of the reasons why she had never moved away from Michigan to another state.

"We have lots of rivers, and there are quite a few lakes if you visit the eastern side of the state." The young woman spoke proudly. "But, of course, no lakes as big as Lake Michigan."

"I guess I didn't explore enough of Kansas. I'm glad you have had a chance to see Lake Michigan."

"Do you think you could get some of those flowers in the picture?"

"Sure. Why don't you stand there?" Emily pointed to a carpet of spring beauties beside a tall paper birch tree. The couple stood by the tree with their arms around each other and smiled toward the camera.

Emily smiled at their happy faces, took a couple of pictures, and handed the phone back to the woman.

The woman showed them to the man. "Those are great. Thank you."

"You're welcome."

As Emily started walking back down the trail toward the parking lot, the couple walked along with her. The young woman walked beside her, while the young man walked close behind them. Emily hiked at a fast pace, knowing she needed to get to her car and drive to work. She didn't want to appear to be unfriendly to the couple, so she tried to answer their questions as she hiked. She sometimes felt that she spent a lot of time during the day explaining things and answering questions. Most of the time she loved her job and the questions and explanations, but on her off time she preferred not to feel like she was working.

"What other hikes would you recommend? Where we can see Lake Michigan, like this trail."

"There is the Bluffs Trail. It's a bit south from the Cliffs Trail and provides a great view of the lake from a different perspective. If you stop at the National Park Office, you could get a map that will show you many of the different hikes in the area."

"That would be helpful. The Park Office was where we bought the sweatshirts." The young woman pointed to the white sweatshirt she was wearing. "It was much colder here at night than we thought it would be. We didn't think to ask about a trail map when we bought them. Our friends told us about this hike, so we decided to start with that."

Emily nodded and kept walking. She heard voices of people coming up the trail toward them, adult voices and a child's voice. When their group approached, Emily guessed the group included two grandparents, a young dad with a baby on his back, and a young mother holding a young child's hand while he hopped along beside her. Emily stepped off the trail to let them pass, and the young couple followed her example.

The dad nodded. "Nice day for a hike."

"Yes, it's great." Emily nodded back.

After the group passed by them, Emily and the couple continued on down the trail, passing through an area with several large trees lying on the ground, crossed on top of each other. Some of them looked like they had snapped off at the top, while others had seemed to have toppled over as if they had been yanked out by the roots.

The young woman gestured to the trees on both sides of the trail. "What happened to all of those trees?"

"There was a big windstorm in 2015 that blew through here and toppled a lot of big trees. Other trees fell down in other storms, or from old age or disease. You can see where smaller trees are starting to grow up to take their places."

"How do you know so much about this area?"

"I work at the Nature Center. Every time I hike somewhere, I notice something new."

The young man nodded. "We try to learn about the places we visit." He laughed. "That's why we ask so many questions."

Emily smiled at him.

"We are staying at a B&B in town. Do you have a favorite restaurant?" The young woman looked at Emily, keeping up the hiking pace that she set.

"There are a lot of great places to eat downtown. It depends on what you like. There are restaurants for seafood, veggie, sushi, Italian, fusion, pizza."

"Lots of choices."

When the three of them got to the parking area, there were more cars than when Emily had arrived earlier. A busy day at the trail, she thought. The unusually warm spring weather encouraged people to get outside. Emily said goodbye to the couple and hoped they enjoyed their stay in the area. They thanked her and waved.

Emily got into her car, turned right out of the parking lot, and sped down the road toward town. She didn't notice the car that tried to follow her but remained stuck behind cars waiting to turn left onto the highway.

The couple from Kansas sat in their car. The car ahead of them waited to turn left. Sitting in the passenger seat, the young woman posted the photo of them taken in front of the tree to let their friends and family know they were enjoying themselves.

The young man turned his head as someone knocked on the window. A man of about thirty, in a navy, hooded sweatshirt and sunglasses, smiled at him in a friendly way. The young man rolled down the window.

"Sorry to bother you, but I noticed that your left rear tire looks like it's low on air. I always keep an air gauge in my car, and I would be happy to check your tire for you. I wouldn't want you to get on the highway and have a flat tire." The man held up his air gauge.

"That's really nice of you. Thanks. This is a rental car, so I thought they would check the tires before they rented it to us. Oh, well, you never know if things are checked out or not."

"Looks like you came up from Kansas."

"Yes, It's beautiful here. Our friends recommended it because we wanted to see the Great Lakes."

"Yes, it's a nice area. Your friend who took a picture of you is a professional photographer? Looked like she had a nice camera."

The young couple smiled. "We just met her today. She takes photos for the Nature Center."

"It'll just take me a minute to check your tire. I'll be right back."

The young man nodded. A couple of minutes later the man in the hoodie came back to the window.

"It's a bit low, but I think you should be fine. You might want to check it in town before you head back to Kansas, though."

"Thanks. Glad to know it's okay." The young man rolled up the window. The man in the hoodie walked back to his car and got in. The car turning left saw a clear spot and turned. The couple from Kansas pulled out onto the road and headed back toward town.

The young woman smiled at the young man. "That was very kind of him. People seem very friendly and helpful up here, don't you think?"

"Seems so. Glad the tire isn't going to go flat."

"I think we should check the tires, though. When we go past a gas station with an air pump, maybe we should see how much air we need."

"Okay. Watch to see if there is one."

On their way back to the city, they drove through a small town that had a small grocery store with a gas station. Driving slowly, the young man spotted an air pump on the side of the building. He pulled the car up to it and used the gauge to check the air in the rear tires. The young woman got out of the car and watched him.

"All the tires seem okay." The young man hung up the air hose and looked at the tires.

"Must have just been how the car was sitting that it looked a bit low to that guy. On a hill or something."

"Well, it all seems okay." They got into the car and drove back to the city.

Chapter 2

When Emily entered the Nature Center, Sara waved to her. Sara staffed the reception counter and did the office work. She had grown up in northern Michigan. They had become friends, as well as coworkers.

"Hi, Sara, how's it going today? Has it been busy?" Emily leaned against the counter and looked at the guest book. Several visitors had added their names today.

"We've had some customers asking about the trails. It seems early for tourist season. Guess the warm weather has brought people out. Mrs. Taylor's bio class from the high school should be here soon. She doesn't tolerate any nonsense, so they should be well-behaved and not give you any trouble."

"Glad to hear that. Last week one of the classes I taught was a bit rowdy. I had to work especially hard to keep them focused. Spending so much time keeping them on track always makes me feel that I haven't really taught them anything."

"Not your fault. What's the lesson for today?"

"Managing nature to adapt to climate change. Mrs. Taylor always tries to talk with her students about current issues and how they might be affected by them. I'll take them on a nature walk after the discussion. Talk to you later."

"Good luck. Let me know if you need anything."

"Thanks." Emily walked to the office that she shared with Mike. He was not often in the office, since he was usually out on the trails clearing downed trees that blocked the trail, fixing fences or lookout platforms, clearing out invasive species. His education specialty was trees, and he sometimes made presentations to groups.

She pulled out the folder with the handouts she had prepared for the students and walked to the education room. She arranged the chairs and placed a handout on each chair.

When she heard voices as the students entered the front door, she went out to the entrance to meet them. It was a small class, only 25 students, an advanced class for seniors only. Mrs. Taylor had high expectations for her students, and the seniors who signed up had to meet specific criteria.

Mrs. Taylor ushered the students into the education room and urged them to listen carefully to Miss Thomas. They settled down when Emily went to the front of the room and welcomed them. Emily noted one student who sat in the back, slouched in his chair. His posture and facial expression looked like a challenge.

"Welcome to the Nature Center. Your teacher told me you have already had some discussion about climate change and its effects. First, tell me what you know about climate change. After a brief discussion, we will go out on the trails and look at some of the effects we can already see and think about some of the effects that could happen in the future. So, let's start with a definition of climate change. Ideas?"

Three students raised their hands, and she nodded to one girl sitting in the back row.

"Long-term shifts in temperature and weather patterns. Some of the changes are caused by natural phenomenon, and some are caused by increased levels of carbon dioxide and other phenomenon caused by people."

"Good definition. What are some of the effects we have seen over the last century? You can just call them out as you think of them."

"Hotter temperatures, sometimes severe enough to kill people. More and more serious wildfires."

"Changes in precipitation, either more or less. More and fiercer storms."

"Droughts. Flooding."

"More insects." Some groans.

"Loss of habitats for animals. More animals will probably become extinct."

"What if climate change isn't real?" A voice from the back row. Emily noticed that Mrs. Taylor rolled her eyes but looked straight ahead.

"I would say look at the scientific evidence, notice what is going on around you and in the rest of the world, think how changes have occurred in your life so far. Make up your own mind based on what you find." Emily gave the boy in the back row a friendly smile. He shrugged.

"We are going to go out on the trails to see if we can find evidence of some of the effects that are already happening in the nature area here, and consider future effects that might happen. When we come back in, we will briefly discuss what can be done to slow down climate change. I know you have already discussed these things, but I want to end on a positive note to remind us that there are ways we can help. You can leave your things here if you wish, as they will be safe, but take your jackets. It's okay to bring phones if you want to take pictures, but I think your teacher would not be okay with your using them for anything else."

Mrs. Taylor nodded. "Don't call your mom, but take advantage of the chance to use your phone to take pictures." Some laughter.

Emily led the students outside and showed them the map by the entrance that explained the trail system. One trail entered the woods to the left of the Center, while the main trail started at the end of a short road and continued along the river. The students followed Emily to the entrance of the second trail.

As they walked the trail, Emily pointed out the effects of invasive insects and disease that were eating away at some of the trees, like the American beech trees that were weakened and then fell. They discussed how the level of the river could change with increased precipitation, causing flooding and destruction of habitat for certain plants and animals. Or, conversely, droughts could decrease the water level and dry up crucial wetland habitats. Emily told them about some of the plants and animals in the preserve that might be affected.

As they walked, Emily named some of the wildflowers and identified birds that they saw or whose calls they heard. A couple of students spotted two pileated woodpeckers sitting on the same tree. Pileated woodpeckers were not unusual here, but it was always interesting to see them, and a special treat to see two perched so close together on the same tree.

When the group returned to the Center, Emily asked them what they were doing or thought they could be doing in their own lives to limit climate change. The students shared the things they did that they hoped had some effect: recycle; find new uses for things, like using found items to create art projects or build things; don't buy things they don't need; donate items they had outgrown or don't use; take public transportation or ride bicycles. Several students expressed frustration that the things they could do would not be enough. They thought that a more universal effort was needed to make the big changes that would be required.

Emily thanked them for coming and for contributing to the discussion. She encouraged them to come back anytime and hike the trails.

As the students left to get back on the bus, some of them stopped to thank Emily. A couple of them asked her how they could get a job doing what she did. She told them about her education and suggested they take as many science classes as they could. Maybe volunteer at the Botanic Garden or one of the Nature Conservancies.

After the class had left, she straightened up the education room and put some things away. She was amazed at how knowledgeable some of the kids were about climate change and how anxious they felt about what would happen in the future. Her generation went to school when teachers were starting to teach more about climate change. She and her friends learned to Reduce, Reuse, Recycle. The world had gotten even more complicated now, as people became more aware of the issues. Some of the students seemed to realize that doing something about climate change is urgent.

Sara had already left to pick up her daughter by the time Emily was ready to go home. She saw Mike going down the hall toward Brad's office. He called out goodbye to her, and she waved back.

On her way home Emily stopped to buy a few groceries and drove to her apartment. When she entered the main door to the building, Reid, her six-year-old neighbor who lived downstairs, was waiting for her by his apartment door. He was slim with curly dark brown hair. He stopped playing with the two action figures he held in his hands and looked up eagerly when she came in.

Reid lived with his mom, who worked until 5:00 Monday through Friday. Reid's grandmother picked him up every day after school. His grandmother sometimes took him home to her house or out on an excursion somewhere, like the library. Other times, like today, she brought him home to his apartment.

On those days, if his grandmother was busy with something in the apartment, Reid waited by his apartment door to intercept Emily when she came home and persuade her to let him see Carson, her cat.

The first time Reid met Carson was soon after Emily had moved into her apartment. Carson slipped out the apartment door, which was not quite closed, and headed downstairs. When Emily discovered the door was ajar and her cat was missing, she ran down the stairs. She found him in the entryway. Reid sat on the floor, petting Carson and talking to him. The cat purred, pleased that he had found a new friend.

Emily told Reid how she had adopted Carson. She worked out with his grandmother that Reid could sometimes visit Carson when Emily got home from work. His grandmother had limited those visits to thirty minutes, as she didn't want to inconvenience Emily. Emily didn't mind the occasional visits. She enjoyed listening to Reid's stories about first grade, and he kept both her and Carson entertained.

Reid broke out into a big smile. "Hi, Emily. You're home. I bet Carson probably wants to see me. He gets lonely during the day, you know."

"Yes, he certainly does." Emily looked serious. "I'll bet he's thinking right now that he wishes Reid would come up to see him soon."

"Do you think so? We'd better go on up, then." Reid started up the stairs.

"Wait a minute, Reid. Don't forget to ask your grandmother first."

Reid came back down the stairs and went into his apartment. Soon his grandmother came out into the hallway. She did not look like the stereotype of a grandma. Reid's mom was young, and Emily figured his grandmother was maybe 50, medium build with brown hair, dressed in slim jeans and a sweater.

"Oh, Emily, you know you don't have to oblige him every day. You must be tired from working."

"It's okay, Mrs. Parker, really. Carson does enjoy the attention. And it's a change for me. We'll just go up for thirty minutes."

"Well, as long as you know you can always say no to him." She looked at Reid. "You be sure and behave yourself and mind Miss Emily."

Reid nodded and started up the stairs ahead of Emily. He stood by her apartment door, bouncing on his feet with excitement.

When Emily and Reid entered the apartment, Carson, her large white cat, jumped down off the refrigerator. He rubbed against both of them and then ran to his food dish. Emily opened a can of food for him and allowed Reid to put just the right amount into the dish. While Emily put the groceries away, Reid pulled a granola bar out of his pocket and began eating while he watched Carson eat his cat food.

When Carson finished eating, Reid stood up and walked over to where Emily stood. "You forgot to ask me about first grade."

Emily put down the groceries and looked at Reid. It was a routine he had initiated when he first came to visit that she should ask him this question. "Oh, I'm sorry, guess I forgot. How was first grade today?"

"It was amazing. A giant snake and an iguana and a turtle all came to visit us." Reid's eyes grew bigger.

"How did they get into your classroom?"

"Well, they didn't just open the door and walk in, did they?" Reid laughed, making Emily smile. "Some woman brought them with her. And she went around the room so we could feel how the snake squeezes its muscles."

"Was it a boa constrictor?"

"That's the one. I was a little afraid of it at first, but when she put it around me, it just squeezed a little bit. She brought the iguana around for us to look at, too, but it didn't have big muscles. And the turtle was kinda shy and mostly hid in its shell. But that woman told us all about them."

"Wow, that does sound like fun."

"The boa and the iguana don't live around here, you know, 'cause they can't take the winters. There are turtles around here, though."

"Sounds like you learned a lot about them."

Reid nodded. He watched Carson wash his face and paws. Then he got out Carson's mouse on a wire toy and played with him until Emily told him his thirty minutes were up, and his grandmother would be waiting for him.

Reid put the toy away. "Sorry to leave you, but I'll see you soon." He petted the cat from head to tail, and said goodbye.

As he opened the door, Reid turned. "If my grandpa can get off work sometime, he's going to pick me up from school and come here and meet Carson. I told Grandpa all about him and how he likes to play with his mouse."

"I'm sure Carson would like to meet your grandpa. See you later."

"See ya." Reid closed the door and went downstairs. Emily opened the door and watched him to be sure he made it safely into his apartment.

Emily ate a salad and some reheated leftovers for dinner. She cleaned up the kitchen and sat on the sofa in the living room to look through the wildflower pictures she had taken on the trails. She and Mike were planning to put together a nature identification book about the area. Her degree was in botany and ecology, and she would be responsible for the entries on flowers and birds. She expected to rely on experienced birders for pictures of some of the birds, but she wanted the flower pictures to be her own photos.

Carson draped himself across her lap and nudged her hand to make sure she didn't ignore him. Before going to bed she texted Ryan. "Hi. Had a good day at the Center. Good luck with the dissert mtg tomorrow. Miss you."

He texted back right away. "Out w/friends. Miss you too. Glad your day went well. See u tomorrow nite."

Emily felt pleasantly tired from a successful day. She missed sharing it with Ryan and would be glad to see him tomorrow. Carson jumped up on the bed and curled up beside her.

Chapter 3

Thursday

At the end of the day, Emily walked down the hall to see if she could talk to Brad. She wanted to suggest that the Center hire a member of the Anishinaabe to give a presentation on the plants that they use for healing. She was eager to learn more about native plants that could be used as medicine. Brad's door was closed, and she heard his voice in a one-sided conversation as if he were on the phone. She would have to catch him tomorrow. If he said it was okay, she would visit the Museum and Cultural Center and see if they could recommend someone who might give a presentation.

Sara was busy with a small group of hikers who wanted to know about the trails, so Emily waved to her and left. Just a couple of cars and an SUV were still in the parking lot. A man in a hoodie stood beside the SUV looking at his phone. He did not look up as she walked by.

Just after she got into her car and turned the key, Ryan texted her that he was on his way home and expected to be there by 9:00. She texted back, "Great. Drive carefully. Miss you."

Emily drove her car into the parking lot of the Loon Lake Trail Nature Area. She was delighted to see that there were no other cars parked in the lot. She would have the trail to herself, at least for a while. This trail had opened up last week after the Conservancy volunteers had cleared it. Probably not many people knew about it yet. She would enjoy the peace and quiet after the busyness at the Cliffs Trail yesterday. She liked to share this beautiful area in Northern Michigan with people who appreciated it, but sometimes she preferred winter hiking, when the trails were quieter.

Since Ryan wouldn't be back in town until later tonight, she had decided to take a hike before going back to her apartment. Spring was when she needed to take photographs of wildflowers, and different ones grew on different trails. She was trying to hike as many of the trails in the area as she could to find the flowers that she had not yet photographed for the nature book.

She got out of her car, put her snack bag in her jacket pocket, grabbed her water bottle, and put the camera strap around her neck. Her phone was still in her backpack in the back seat. She wouldn't need it and liked to hike sometimes without it. When she took people on hikes, she always had it with her in case there was an emergency. It felt good to be disconnected from the world for a while.

The air was already cooling off near the end of the day, but the sunshine warmed her. The temperatures of the past couple of days had been warmer than usual for spring, and she enjoyed it. She breathed in the scent of flowers, evergreen trees, and the freshness of spring, new beginnings.

The trail map on the sign showed a loop trail about two miles long, curving around past the lake. Daylight was lasting a little longer each day. It was already 4:00, but she would make it back to the car well before dark. She liked hiking at night, but didn't do it alone or often.

She followed the arrow to the right and headed across a flat, grassy area. The blooms of dutchman's breeches were fading. Some of the wild columbine were budded and others were beginning to open. Small pine trees that had sprouted on their own poked up through the grass at random. Up ahead, the trail climbed slightly into the woods. Leaf buds opening on maple and oak trees created a bright-green haze high up in the trees. One of her favorite flowers, the white trillium, spread a beautiful carpet of frilly blossoms throughout the woods.

Enjoying the fresh air, the rhythm of hiking, and the sounds of the woods, Emily felt the tension of the day ebb away. It hadn't been a bad day, just one of those days that took extra energy. She had worked with a group of middle schoolers, teaching them how to identify trees. Mike often did the tree hikes, but he hadn't been available today. A couple of students kept goofing off and distracted the rest of the group. She finally coaxed those two out of their attitudes, and they settled down. Some kids seemed to need to get themselves noticed before they could join in with the group.

Emily looked forward to her day-off from work tomorrow. Her sister was coming to visit her from Chicago. Candace sometimes played the "older sister" role a bit too much, but she was fun and made Emily laugh. She also reminded Emily of home. Most of the time Emily felt she had settled in up here, but lately she felt a bit homesick.

Next week was the anniversary of her father's death. He had been so healthy and active while she and her sister were growing up. Then suddenly he found out he had cancer and died within three months. Candace, Emily, and their mom felt his absence acutely. After he died the three of them became a very close unit, always looking out for each other.

Candace had not wanted to go off to university, because she felt responsible for Emily and their mom. But their mom insisted that she go, and pulled herself together quickly to provide some stability for her two daughters. Candace went to the East Coast to university, but Emily stayed in the Midwest and attended the University of Michigan to be close to her mom. Her mom still missed their dad, Emily knew, but she had created a new life for herself after their dad died. Emily thought there might even be a new man in the picture, but her mom hadn't said anything about that yet.

It had been many years since her dad died, but Emily always had her own quiet moment of remembrance on the anniversary of his death. This year, perhaps because she had moved farther away from home, she felt his absence more strongly.

When she first moved up here, she felt lucky to have gotten the job at the Nature Center because such jobs were hard to find. This was the kind of job she wanted. She knew it was a risk to move up north because she didn't know anyone here. But people had been friendly, and she figured she would get to know people as time went on.

And finding her cat, Carson, had helped. One day she had been talking to Sara while they waited for a staff meeting. A copy of the local paper was lying on the counter, turned to the page where the Humane Society featured animals for adoption every Thursday. As she looked at the animals on the page, the picture of a white cat, whose name was Snowflake, caught her attention. His description said he had been rescued from an unethical breeder. He was described as quiet, but affectionate when he got to know you. For some reason, she felt that he needed her, and she called the Humane Society to ask when she could meet him.

The next afternoon she went there and was allowed to take him out of his cage. He was a bit thin, but soft and plushy. He immediately put his front paws on her shoulders and snuggled against her. Emily adopted him right then. The woman at the Humane Society had asked a lot of questions about how she would care for Snowflake, since she lived by herself in a small apartment. But she had grown up with a beloved cat, clearly Carson, aka Snowflake, approved of her, and the Humane Society had a large number of cats to find homes for. So, she passed the test and was allowed to adopt the cat.

Since she didn't have any cat supplies, she stopped at a pet store on her way home and bought what she would need. The next day she brought Snowflake home to her apartment. The name Snowflake didn't seem to suit him, and since the Humane Society had given him that name, he wasn't attached to it. And so, she named him Carson. In Maine she had walked the boardwalk trails at the Rachel Carson Preserve, and thought the name Carson suited him.

As soon as she let Carson out of the carrier in her apartment, he explored every inch of it, making the place his own. Over the next few weeks, Carson put on some weight and became more energetic. It turned out that he considered himself an athlete and continued to challenge himself to reach all of the spaces in the apartment. Emily was no longer homesick, and when Ryan moved here, it felt more like home.

On a path off to the right of the main trail, Emily walked to Loon Lake. It was a small, oval-shaped lake, surrounded by a mix of hardwoods and pines. Without much breeze, the smooth water reflected the trees around it. At the far end a creek flowed into the lake through a grassy inlet.

Sitting on a log, she pulled out her snack bag and nibbled on some walnuts and figs. The eerie wail of loons alerted her to a pair of them swimming and diving in the middle of the lake. She smiled as two little loons popped up nearby and looked around for their parents. She waited for the right moment when all four of the loons swam together and got a good close-up photo of the family.

She thought about the discussion she'd had with Ryan the night before last. She had asked him if there was something on his mind because he seemed so distracted lately. He assured her that he was fine, but he was having second thoughts about his dissertation subject. Since he was already halfway into the writing of it, he was worried he wouldn't finish it and all that time would be wasted. What would he do then? Had his work on it been a waste of time? Was he just putting off deciding what direction to go in?

He surprised her when he suggested that they move in together. They would have more time together and could save money toward buying a place. It was true that they already practically lived together. Sharing the rent would certainly help financially. Rent, a car payment, and a small student loan made things tight.

But she had hedged a bit, just not sure she was ready. In part because she wasn't sure what would happen when he finished his dissertation. She knew she wanted to stay at the Nature Center, but Ryan might want a job somewhere else. He seemed hurt when she didn't commit to his idea. She hoped he had gotten encouragement from his dissertation committee so that he felt on track to finish writing it.

She stood up and continued hiking on the main trail, past several fallen trees with vines tumbling over them and new green ferns unfurling nearby. Two squirrels chased each other back and forth through the rustling leaves that still covered the ground from last fall.

Emily stopped and looked at a trail off to the left of the main trail. It looked unused, like it wasn't part of the main trail system. It was one of those trails she always thought looked intriguing but she didn't take. She would have time to walk partway down it and see where it might lead. Then she could come back when she had more time to finish hiking it.

Ferns poked up in the trail, and large tree roots snaked across it. Some large oak and maple trees provided an expansive canopy, while their dried leaves carpeted the path, hiding the roots. Looking around at the greenery, she caught herself just in time from tripping over one gnarled root. Best to keep a closer watch on her feet.

Out of the corner of her eye she spied a patch of blue flowers she had not seen in the woods this spring. She stopped and looked at them closely. They looked like hepatica. Six petals, three rounded leaves, right time of the year for them to bloom. She hadn't seen blue ones in the woods before, just white ones. She would look it up to be sure she was right, when she got back to her apartment. She knelt down, zoomed the camera lens in closely, and took a picture.

She heard a snuffling sound ahead of her and stood up quickly. About fifty yards ahead stood a black bear. She froze, startled. She took a deep breath. The bear was beautiful, majestic. The bear turned its head and looked right at her. Seeing the bear was unexpected, but she was not really afraid. She knew that black bears didn't usually attack people. It was spring, though, and it could be a female with cubs nearby that it would protect.

She started backing up slowly, remembering the camping trip she took in Glacier National Park with her parents and her sister the summer before Emily started eighth grade. They hiked on trails that warned them to be careful in "grizzly country." As a precaution, their dad took them to a presentation about encountering bears. Black bears avoid people as much as possible and seldom attack anybody. The ranger advised them not to run, back away slowly. If attacked by a black bear, fight back. If attacked by a grizzly, play dead and hope for the best. Emily had been a bit disappointed that they did not encounter any bears on that trip. Although grizzlies were probably best seen from a distance. So, it was an unexpected treat to finally see a bear in the wild. Still, she didn't want to take chances.

"Look big," the park ranger had said. She opened her arms wide. "Make noise." She began to sing, "The bear went over the mountain, the bear went over the mountain." The bear stood still, stared.

She heard rustlings in the leaves behind her. The squirrels hadn't spotted the bear or weren't afraid of it. Suddenly, the bear began to move toward her.

Four Hours Later

Emily opened her eyes. She must have been asleep. Why would she be asleep out here? It was dark in the woods, cloudy, no moon brightening the sky and no visible stars. She lay curled up on her side on ground covered with pine needles. What was she doing here in this low depression underneath a pine tree? Something rustled in the undergrowth back in the woods, and she tried to curl up smaller so as not to be seen. What was out there?

There was a sharp pain in her head. Why did it hurt so much? She put her hand up to her head and felt a large bump on the back of it. How did she get a bump on her head? When she stretched her legs, she yelped as she experienced the pain in her left ankle. Was it broken? She felt her arms and legs. She didn't seem to have any wounds, just some bruises, maybe.

What had happened? She must have been hiking on a trail somewhere. What trail would she have been on? She couldn't have walked here, so she must have left her car somewhere. She should get up and walk back to her car. When she looked around her, she could see that the darkness was almost absolute. Her phone would have a flashlight. She felt in her jacket pockets. No phone. Her camera was still around her neck. She took it off and laid it next to her.

Why didn't she remember what had happened? She shook her head, but that only made it hurt more. The most important task was to get out of the woods. As she looked around her, the trees seemed to be closing in on her. Without houses or buildings nearby, no lights shone in the distance.

Clearly, she couldn't walk out of here while it was so dark. She wouldn't be able to see where she was going, and she felt disoriented about where she actually was. The woods had always seemed friendly to her, but right now it seemed that dangers lurked. She would have to wait until daylight to find her way out of the woods. She should try to sleep, but sleeping seemed impossible.

She heard an eerie sound in the distance. A barred owl, maybe. Another owl answered the call from across the woods. The sound was familiar, comforting somehow.

She realized that she had been dreaming before she opened her eyes. She dreamed that Ryan lay beside her, keeping her warm. Her back did feel warm, while her front felt cold. To cheer herself up, she thought about Ryan.

When she first met him, she was taking pictures of flowers at the Botanical Garden in Ann Arbor. He was looking at his phone while walking on the path in the outside garden. Not seeing her kneeling to take a picture, he almost knocked her over. Just in time he grasped her arm and kept her from falling. She frowned in annoyance until she looked up into his warm brown eyes, curly brown hair falling over his forehead. He looked so concerned and apologized so much, she couldn't be annoyed with him. Not only was he very good-looking, he seemed sincere and kind.

She told him to stop apologizing, no harm done, and he suggested having coffee at the Botanical Garden's café. She usually turned down pick-up invitations from strangers, but something about him made it seem okay. Drinking coffee and talking, they discovered they both wanted to travel, liked the same kind of music, enjoyed outdoor activities, and wanted to publish a book someday.

After having coffee, they exchanged phone numbers. She didn't know if she would ever contact him, although she was interested. But he called the next day and suggested they take a walk at the Arboretum. Conversation came easily, as if they had known each other for longer than a couple of days. Seeing each other became a regular thing.

Did Ryan know she was out here in the woods? Would he be looking for her? She closed her eyes, wanting to forget the pain in her head and go back to dreaming. Sleep eluded her for a long time. Every time she closed her eyes, the rustlings in the forest made her cringe. The ground was uncomfortable, and she shivered from the cold. She shifted positions, tried deep breathing. Although she felt tired, she didn't want to close her eyes. She wished she were home in bed.

It was getting dark when Ryan drove his car into the parking lot of his apartment building. He lived in a two-story brick building with a narrow porch across the front. It was divided into four apartments, two downstairs and two upstairs. Ryan's apartment was downstairs.

He grabbed his travel bag and walked around to the front of the building. Mike and Zac, who had the apartment next to Ryan's, sat on the porch steps drinking a couple of beers. Mike worked with Emily, and Zac worked at one of the wineries on the Peninsula. Ryan had Mike to thank for finding his apartment. Apartments were hard to come by, and he had spent a lot of time looking for one. When Mike had told Emily that the apartment next to his and Zac's would be vacant when the current tenants moved out, Emily nabbed the apartment for Ryan.

"Hey, Ryan. Where you been off to? Beer?" Mike picked up a bottle from the porch and held it out to Ryan.

"Hey, Mike, Zac. A cold beer sounds good. I went down to Ann Arbor to take care of some things."

"Back to your old stomping ground. A good trip?"

"Something like that. It was good to be back in Ann Arbor, but I'm glad to be home, too."

"Emily didn't go with you?"

"No, not this time. She had lots going on at the Nature Center. You and she are working on that guidebook for one thing. Her sister is coming up from Chicago tomorrow, and she wanted to get things done so she could take off a couple of days to spend with her."

"She talks about Candace sometimes. Big sister and all that."

"Emily is kind of in awe of Candace, I think. So, how're things going at the winery, Zac? Grapes doing okay with this weather?"

"Looks like it's going to be a good year in spite of the hot/cold back and forth that keeps us guessing. I'm hoping some new vines we planted will produce this year.

"Good luck with that." Ryan sat on the step and sipped his beer.

"What do you think of the Tigers? They've gotten off to a slow start, but have potential." Mike and Zac were big Detroit Tigers fans, so they had lots to say about how the season was shaping up.

"I check the game results but don't know that much about the new players. Looks like a couple of new pitchers since last year."

Mike and Zac began discussing the pros and cons of several players. Ryan listened to their back and forth. They seemed like a tight couple, but weren't afraid to disagree.

Seemed like he and Emily seldom argued. Was that a good thing? He finished his beer, and stood up.

"Thanks for the beer. I'd better text Emily and let her know I'm here. Catch you later."

"See you around. Come on over to watch a game sometime."

"Will do."

Ryan went into his apartment and put some things away. He sat down and texted Emily. "Just got home. Coming over?"

He turned on the television but realized he wasn't really paying attention to what he was watching. His mind was elsewhere. Seemed like Emily would have responded by now. He understood if she was out with Candace and couldn't make it over, but she could at least let him know. He stood up and stretched. No need to get worked up over nothing. He would get an early night and be up early in the morning to get going on his writing. He would see Emily tomorrow.

Chapter 4

Friday

The alarm rang at 5:00 a.m. Candace rolled over and put her arms around Josh, who hadn't stirred at the sound of the alarm. One of the disadvantages of spending the night with a successful chef was the early morning hours he kept to do prep work and experiment with recipes when no one else was in the restaurant kitchen.

Josh groaned, then rolled over and gave her a long kiss. One of the advantages of spending the night with a successful chef was Josh himself. His family wasn't poor, but money had always been tight. His parents had both worked hard to make sure he and his two older sisters could attend college. The three of them went to community college and lived at home for the first two years, then each transferred to a four-year college.

Josh wanted to help out his parents so they could stop working and retire someday. Although it wasn't his favorite subject, he was good at math, so he became a Certified Public Accountant. For several years he worked, saved up his money, and helped to pay off his parents' mortgage. Working at different jobs, his sisters helped as much as they could.

Josh had always loved to cook and tried out his gourmet creations on his friends and family. His parents could see he wasn't happy as a CPA. They told him he should do what he really wanted to do and stop worrying about them. He quit his job, went to chef's school, and took advantage of every opportunity to learn as much as he could about cooking.

Candace appreciated that he knew who he was and what he wanted. No mystery, no complications. Josh was always Josh. It also didn't hurt that growing up with two older sisters had taught him the benefits of respecting women.

"Do you have to get up?" Candace sighed.

"Soon. But you said you wanted to get an early start today, since you're going to see Emily, so we both need to get up."

"Getting up early sounded like a good idea at the time." She snuggled next to him and closed her eyes. Then she opened them. She had promised Emily she would be there in time for lunch. Emily would be expecting her, and Emily was always on time. "Okay, guess it's time to get a shower and get going."

The shower took a bit longer than expected, but soon they were both dressed and sitting at the kitchen counter drinking coffee and eating toasted bagels. Josh ate hurriedly, kissed the back of Candace's neck, and told her to text him when she got to Emily's apartment.

Candace packed a travel bag with what she might need for a couple of days, put her phone in her purse, and locked the apartment door. She found Josh's Miata parked on the street outside the apartment. Candace didn't own a car and always took public transportation in the city. When she left the city, she either flew or rented a car.

When she made a last-minute decision to visit Emily, she planned to rent a car, rather than fly, since she would want a car while she was there. But Josh said he hardly ever used the Miata and he would be grateful if she took it for a long drive. She was a careful driver but felt a bit nervous driving his car.

Josh convinced her it would be fine, and she couldn't resist having the Miata for a few days. She was glad she had gotten up early after all. Driving out of Chicago was always a challenge, and leaving early in the morning was the best bet.

Crossing into Michigan after passing through a small part of Indiana, Candace smiled at the "Pure Michigan" sign that welcomed her. She and Emily had grown up in a suburb of Detroit, but Candace had spent several years on the East Coast attending University. After graduation she had interned at a couple of museums, while working as a barista in a coffee shop to support herself. Finally, she landed the job at the Art Institute of Chicago. She loved Chicago, the big city, with all the culture and entertainment, interesting people. Still, when she entered Michigan, she had a sense of being home. This was the second time she had driven up north to visit Emily. Usually, being in Michigan meant taking I94 across to the southeast to visit her mom.

She still had a long way to drive, so she turned on the radio and tuned into a favorite station. She sang along to the songs that she knew and tapped out the rhythm when she didn't know the words. In high school she had imagined herself singing in a famous rock band. While she was in college, she sang with a local band for a few months, but the band members weren't very serious, and the band broke up pretty quickly. A lost opportunity.

She pulled off the highway only once at a rest stop and was quickly back on the road. It was early on a Friday in the spring, so traffic wasn't heavy, and she made good time. In a few hours, she was off the freeway and traveling on two-lane roads through northern Michigan.

Candace always wondered what made her sister move up to the north, away from civilization. When she drove around the Bay, she could see some of the attraction. She drove through the downtown to see what it was like. She decided it was pretty cute, with cafes where you could get real coffee, a couple of good bookstores, a movie theater, and some interesting shops. To Candace those were signs of real civilization.

When Emily had texted her that she had today off work, Candace decided it was time to visit her sister. She hadn't come up to see Emily since last fall, and hadn't seen her since Christmas. She missed her little sister, not so little, as they were only 18 months apart in age. But she always felt protective, as if Emily were too kind and sensitive for the big, bad world.

Once when they were kids, they found an injured bird lying on the sidewalk in front of their house. Even then Emily could identify it as a Baltimore Oriole, black with that brilliant orange. The bird was still alive, and Emily had been adamant that they had to find someone to fix it. Candace had called the Humane Society, which referred her to a bird rescue lady. Candace called her, and the two of them sat with the bird while Emily hummed a tune to "keep it company," as they waited for the woman to pick it up. They never heard if the bird had made it.

As they grew up, she and Emily looked out for each other but moved in different directions. Emily continued to study birds and trees and animals. She even started a small garden in the backyard of their house. Candace was more interested in clothes and music and boys. They had each found their niche, she guessed, and were still friends. Also, clearly Emily was more interested in boys these days. She had fallen for Ryan pretty fast, and that seemed to be working out.

Candace pulled over to text Emily that she was getting close to her apartment. She waited a couple of minutes, but got no response. She frowned. She had told Emily about when she expected to arrive, and she usually texted before she finally got there. She waited a few more minutes, but still received no response. She drove on to Emily's apartment, deciding she would just surprise her.

Emily lived in Apartment 4 in an old Victorian house, white with dark blue trim, that had been divided into four apartments. Her apartment was on the second floor, facing the backyard. Candace parked on the street and pushed the buzzer by the front door for Emily's apartment. No one answered. She tried the other two buzzers, hoping someone would let her in. She got no answer from either of them. Emily had told her that the fourth apartment was being rehabbed and a piece of tape had been placed over its buzzer. Candace texted Emily again and then phoned, but the call just went to voice mail.

Emily's car was not in the driveway or along the street. That was annoying. She had told Emily about when to expect her. Her sister was so reliable. She wouldn't leave without texting Candace to let her know that she wasn't going to be at her apartment. Maybe Emily had stayed with Ryan last night and overslept or something. Candace checked her phone for his address. His apartment wasn't far, at least not compared to the distances Candace was used to in the Chicago area. A short drive with a few turns through town and she would be there.

Daylight filtered through the pine boughs. Emily woke up again, panicked. She looked around, wondering where she was. She must have finally fallen asleep. She needed to get up, find her way back to her car. She sat up suddenly, felt dizzy and nauseous, and lay back down. The ground was hard and cold. Something softer would have helped her head feel better. She curled up and tried to snuggle into the pine needles to get warmer.

She sensed the rush of something moving nearby and looked up suddenly. A few yards away a red fox stopped in his tracks and stared at her. He was beautiful, his bright red coat striking against the green trees.

"Wow, look at you." Emily spoke quietly, staring back at the fox.

Just as suddenly as he had appeared, the fox turned and darted off in the other direction, away from her. Emily just sat for a minute, awed that she had seen a fox so close to her. She shook her head, gently. Seeing the fox was amazing, but she was stuck here in the woods and had to figure out what to do.

Sun peeking through the pine boughs hurt her eyes, but she craved its warmth after a cold night. She crawled closer to the trunk of the tree and slumped against it. What had happened to her? Why was she here? And why did she feel so terrible?

She was hungry and thirsty. She must have dropped her water bottle somewhere. No hope for ending her thirst. She felt in her jacket pocket and found the bag of snacks. She must have eaten some before she ended up here, as there wasn't much left, but there were a couple of figs and a few nuts, even a couple of chocolate covered coffee beans. Should she eat all of it or save some for later? She didn't plan to be here long. She had her keys, she would find her car and drive home.

Had Ryan come home last night? Was he worried? Was he looking for her?

And wasn't her sister supposed to come? What would Candace think when she didn't find her at her apartment? Why could she remember Ryan and Candace but she couldn't remember what she was doing here?

She decided to eat all of the snacks. As soon as she stopped feeling dizzy, she would get up and find her way back to where she had parked her car. She could do this.

Ryan woke up with the sun dappling the floor through the gap in the curtains. He had overslept. He intended to get an early start on writing today. This wasn't the first time he had intended to do so. But the meeting yesterday with his dissertation committee had gone well, and he was determined to finish it and get on with his life.

When he had complained to Emily about his lack of focus on the dissertation, she had reminded him that he didn't have to let it define his life. She told him to finish it and get his degree. Then he could do anything he wanted. What that would be, he wasn't sure. Teaching might work out. He had been a Teaching Assistant at the University, and mostly enjoyed it. Except he didn't like giving grades or the politics of tenure, if getting a job with tenure was even an option these days. Research, maybe. First things first. Finish the dissertation.

Whatever he did, he hoped Emily would be part of his life. She seemed reluctant to move in together right now, but he thought she would change her mind. They met a couple of years ago at the Botanical Garden. Not watching where he was going, he literally bumped into her while she was taking pictures. She was kneeling down with her camera focused on a flower, and he had almost knocked her over. He grasped her arm to keep her from falling, "Sorry, sorry, sorry. I'm so sorry. I wasn't paying attention. Are you okay? I'm an idiot."

And Emily laughed. "No harm done. Enough with so many I'm sorries, although that's some of the best apologizing I've heard."

He smiled and noted how blue her eyes were, how sweet her face. He was impressed that she didn't seem flustered or angry at him for running into her. And she seemed ready to forgive him for it.

He asked her about her photographs. Did she have a gallery to show or sell them somewhere? After they talked about photography, he suggested they have coffee at the café inside the Botanical Garden. To his surprise, she agreed to that. He texted her the next day, and the relationship took off, slowly but surely.

When she told him she had been offered the job at the Nature Center up here, he could tell she really wanted to accept it. He encouraged her to take it and assured her that they could continue their relationship long distance while she decided if she liked the job. He helped her to move in up here, and they talked every night on the phone. On weekends he drove up to see her, or she came down to Ann Arbor. After a couple of months, he decided to move up here while he finished writing his dissertation. He and Emily just felt right together, and he didn't want to lose that.

Not wanting to be overly dependent on her, he got a part-time job at a record store. He made enough money to pay his own expenses while working on his dissertation and got to know a few people. He had never thought he would like a retail job, but he enjoyed helping people find the record they were looking for or try something new. Uncle Mike, his mother's older brother, had a giant vinyl collection that Ryan had often listened chosen records from. The collection included music from classical to jazz to rock and roll. His uncle taught him a lot about the history of music

A couple of weeks ago, he decided to quit the job at the record store and work full time on his dissertation. He wanted that phase of his life over. He would still have the orals to get through, but he would worry about that later. He told himself to stop overthinking everything and start working.

To clear his head, he put on his running clothes, just ordinary ones, not fancy like the serious runners in town. One benefit of moving here was that he discovered cross-country skiing, in particular skate skiing and racing. He ran to keep in shape for winter, when he could cross-country ski. He usually ran through town down to the bay, then along the bay and back home.

He ran track in high school, in part to please his dad, who was an avid sports enthusiast. Ryan enjoyed running, but enjoyed improving his own times more than outrunning someone else. His lack of competitiveness irked his dad, who coached high school football as part of his teaching job. Fortunately, Ryan's older brother was super-competitive and successful as a basketball star. That pleased their dad, gave him someone to cheer for and be proud of.

His mom had a different attitude. After a track meet, she always asked him how he felt about it. If he said he didn't feel he had done his best, she sympathized with how that happens sometimes. If he said he did well, she congratulated him on what he had achieved. She was a lawyer for a non-profit organization, and he figured she must have been competitive to get through law school. But her advice to him was always that she hoped he would try to be kind, do his best, and find what made him happy.

Ryan walked around before returning to his apartment to cool down. He took a quick shower, dressed and made coffee and toast. His apartment was small, but he was lucky to have found it. Emily had told him housing was hard to find, and he had come up more than once to look.

The kitchen/eating area of his apartment was in a small alcove off the main room, which included a couch, two chairs, his desk, and a bookcase. He tried to keep everything in order and stay focused, and mostly it worked. Spreading out his research notes on his desk, he began to organize his thoughts. He was starting a new section and was thinking about how to begin.

Before he started typing into his laptop, he texted Emily to say hello and ask what she and her sister were doing today. She didn't respond, and he was a bit annoyed because she hadn't responded last night either.

When the doorbell rang, he sighed. He didn't need interruptions and thought he might just ignore it. But maybe it was Emily and Candace. He went to the door. Emily's sister stood on the doorstep. She looked distressed, impatient. He wondered what she was doing here without Emily.

Chapter 5

"Hey, Candace. I wasn't expecting you. Where's Emily? I thought you and she were together last night." Ryan stood aside as Candace walked in.

"I wasn't in town last night. I just got here. I'm looking for Emily. Is she here? Did you see her last night? She hasn't answered my texts or calls, but she knew I was coming today. I stopped by her apartment. No answer. Her car wasn't there either." Candace frowned. "Do you know where she is?"

Ryan ran his hand through his hair, waiting for her to slow down. He felt confused. What was he missing here? "I don't know. I thought she was with you. I got back late last night. I texted her that I was back and she could come over, but she didn't answer. I figured you got here yesterday, and you and she were out for a late night. I should have kept trying, maybe gone over there. But I thought that you were here."

"Well, she didn't answer the door at her apartment, and she has today off at work. That's why I came." Candace paced across the living room, paced back again. "When did you last talk to her?"

"We texted back and forth yesterday. I knew she would be busy with a group of middle schoolers in the afternoon, so she wouldn't have time to talk until later. She texted later in the afternoon with just a quick, 'Hi, hope all is going well.' I was headed home from Ann Arbor, so I texted her that I was on my way. She texted back about 4:00. That was the last time I heard from her."

"You didn't talk to her after that? She's missing. We should call the cops, they should be out looking for her."

"They'll just say she hasn't been gone long, she's an adult. Maybe she went out to do some errands, left her phone at home." Ryan tried to convince himself that there was nothing to worry about. But this wasn't like Emily.

"I'm going to call them." Candace was already searching on her phone. "Found the number." When someone answered, she was transferred to a Detective Perez, who sounded underwhelmed with her story of a missing sister. Reluctantly, Candace thought, the detective said she and another detective would come to Ryan's apartment to get more information.

"They're coming over. They'll be here within an hour."

Ryan shook his head. He wasn't at all sure that they needed to involve the cops. He didn't want to sit here waiting, when he needed to be doing something to look for Emily.

"You want a cup of coffee?"

"That would be great. I didn't stop to get coffee on the way up here. I didn't want to take the time. Something doesn't feel right. I wish I'd come yesterday. Then Emily would not be missing." Candace checked her phone again, while Ryan went to the kitchen to get coffee.

"You want milk or straight up?"

"Just black is fine."

Ryan brought two coffees, handed one to Candace, and sat down. He picked up a pen lying on the side table and began clicking it on and off.

Candace paced around the room, glanced at the papers on Ryan's desk. "So, how's the dissertation coming?" She sipped her coffee and set it on the side table.

Ryan wasn't sure if she was really interested, or just trying to fill time while they waited. He felt a bit awkward around Candace. As if she were checking him out as Emily's boyfriend and maybe found him not up to her standards. Candace had gone through more than one boyfriend since he had first met her, so he wasn't sure that she was the best judge of that. "I'm on the last section, I think."

"What's that section about?" Candace walked to the window and then walked back to the other side of the room. She looked at one of the pictures Ryan had put up on the wall.

"I'm researching people who are considered heroes during different historic eras, like the Civil War, the Westward Migration, World War I, World War II, the 1920s, the Depression, the Civil Rights Movements, and today. How people's heroic abilities intersect with the events of particular times. The last section is a comparison of types of heroes valued as times change, and the importance of all the unsung heroes that make any change possible." He grimaced. He sounded like a professor. Every time someone asked him, he automatically gave the same spiel.

"Any heroines?"

"Of course. I use the term 'hero' to apply to each of the people I discuss because I think people tend to react to the term 'heroine' as if it were inferior." Ryan put down the pen. He tapped his foot up and down.

"Makes sense. Then what will you do?" Candace looked out the window, wishing the cops would hurry up and get here. Where was Emily?

"Find a job. Not sure what that will be, but something in this area." Ryan picked up a speckled rock that Emily had found when they were backpacking. She hoped it was a Petoskey stone. It wasn't, but she had kept it. He rolled it back and forth in his hand. "What about you? How's the museum life going in Chicago?"

"We have a new exhibit coming up. Three women who are cutting edge in Contemporary Art." Candace looked at a photo of her and Emily when they were kids, maybe on a family camping trip. They looked tanned and happy.

"Would that be those paintings with a square of one color on a canvas of another color?" He didn't really know much about art, just what he liked or didn't like. Some of it was interesting, creative. Ryan put down the rock.

Candace frowned. "That is what some artists do. There's a lot of creativity in modern art these days, though, and women artists are a big part of it. Contemporary Art is another way of looking at life, challenging you to see something more. You and Emily should come to Chicago and see the exhibit." She stopped, and her eyes grew wide. Emily.

"We'll find her." Ryan's voice was firm. He wanted to get up and get going to make sure that they did find her. "Then we'll visit you in Chicago to see lots of art. Emily would like that. She'll want to see a photographic exhibit as well."

"You're right. We'll find her."

They sat in silence, drinking their coffee, lost in their own thoughts about Emily and what would happen when the cops showed up.

Ryan felt uneasy about the cops coming. When he was sixteen, he and a friend had gone to a party that turned out to be wilder than they had expected. Most of the kids there were definitely underage, and the noise level was loud enough to annoy the neighbors. If he got picked up for underage drinking, his parents would be pretty angry. He and his friend decided to bail out. They dumped out the beer they were getting ready to drink and got into Ryan's car to leave.

As they pulled out of the driveway, a couple of cop cars showed up and blocked them in. Two of the cops headed up toward the party, and two of the cops came up to Ryan's car. They told Ryan and his passenger to get out of the car and questioned them. Ryan and his friend kept insisting that they hadn't been drinking. Finally, after they each took a breathalyzer test, the cops let them go. He had never forgotten the fear that he could be taken to jail, even though he had done nothing wrong. But he told himself, as he sat here waiting, he was older now and could handle the cops.

An hour later there was a knock on the door. Ryan and Candace looked at each other.

Ryan jumped up. "The cops. I'm not sure this is really necessary. Emily might be embarrassed that we told them she was missing."

"Aren't you worried about her?" Candace frowned.

"Of course, I'm worried. But I don't like having the cops involved."

"Just answer the door."

On the doorstep stood a tall man with cropped brown hair. He looked a bit beefy but with muscled arms, as if he worked out. A step behind him stood a woman, of medium height, with dark curly hair, slim, athletic.

"Looking for Ms. Thomas or Mr. Connors. I'm Detective Gibson and this is Detective Perez." The cops took out their IDs and flashed them at Ryan.

"I'm Mr. Connors. Ryan."

"May we come in and talk with you about Emily?"

Polite, respectful. On TV they always start out that way. He opened the door wider, stepped back, and gestured to the couch in the living room. Detective Gibson leaned against the wall while Detective Perez sat on the couch. She looked at Candace, who stood by the window.

"I'm Candace. I'm Emily's sister, older sister. I'm the one who called you."

Detective Perez nodded at Candace, turned back to Ryan. "Are you related to Emily?"

"I'm her boyfriend." Ryan sat in one of the chairs and tried to look calm. Would they think he had hurt Emily? Unthinkable.

"So, tell us about Emily. When did you last see her, and why do you think she might be missing? You said you haven't heard from her for 24 hours? Would that be usual?" Detective Perez crossed her legs, looked at Ryan, then at Candace. Detective Gibson took out his phone and selected an app.

"I got back late last night. I texted her that I was back in town and she could come over, but she didn't answer. I knew Candace was coming to visit her. I figured she and Candace were out for a late night. I thought I would hear from them today."

"Emily doesn't live here then?"

"She has her own apartment, but she sometimes stays here."

"So, you got back late. Where had you been? How long were you there?"

"I drove down to Ann Arbor the night before last. Yesterday morning I had a meeting with my dissertation committee and then stayed to do some research at the library. I met some friends for an early dinner. I texted Emily that I was on my way home, and she texted back about 4:00."

"So, did you see her last night, Candace?" Perez turned to look at Candace, who still stood by the window.

"I drove up from Chicago and got here this morning. I always text Emily when I get close to her apartment. But she didn't answer my text, and she wasn't at her apartment when I got there. We'd planned to meet up and go out to lunch and then go for a hike or something. Emily is always on time. Her car wasn't parked at her apartment, so I came over here to see if she stayed at Ryan's last night. But he hasn't seen her or heard from her either."

"Could she have gone out somewhere early this morning? To the grocery store, for example? Gone for an early hike or a run?"

"No, that isn't like Emily. She's very organized. If she said she would meet me for lunch, that's exactly what she would do. If she had to go out, she would have texted me to let me know. We've always let people know where we are going, since we were kids."

Detective Perez turned back to Ryan. "How were you and Emily getting along? Did you have any arguments recently? Would she be avoiding you, cooling off from some disagreement?"

"No, we don't argue, and Emily isn't like that. She always wants to work things out. If she needed a break to cool down, she would tell me straight up, not leave me wondering where she is."

"So, there was no argument?"

"No, no, not really. We had a discussion the afternoon before I left. She felt I was distracted lately, by the dissertation I'm writing. I wanted us to move in together. I thought we'd have more time with each other. She said she wasn't ready for that. We didn't argue, just talked about it."

"Did you feel rejected that she wouldn't move agree to move in together?"

"Of course not. She'll let me know when she's ready."

"Where might she have gone? Any favorite places? Would she have gone into work on her day off?

"She has lots of favorite hikes. That's her job, really. She works at the Nature Center, assistant director in charge of education. She takes kids on hikes and teaches them about the woods and nature stuff. She's pretty dedicated, but she was looking forward to Candace's coming, so she wouldn't go in to work. She would be here to see her."

"Was she at work yesterday?"

"I think so. I texted her in the afternoon just to say 'Hi,' and she texted back, said she was busy with a group of middle-school students. I guess she might have gone hiking after work. Sometimes she does that, to relax a bit and take wildflower photographs. She talked about a new trail that she wanted to check out. But I have no idea which trail it is." Ryan raked his hand through his hair. "I should have paid more attention to what she said."

"Might she have gotten lost in the woods?"

"That's unlikely. She knows all about getting directions from looking at the position of the sun and all that stuff. She might have gotten hurt, though." He paused. He hadn't really considered that she could be hurt. She seemed so capable in the woods, so at home. "We have to find her. She could be hurt, lying alone somewhere all night!"

Perez noted his seeming anxiety. She looked at Candace. "What about family? Parents? Other siblings? Grandparents? Is there a family member in the area that she might have stopped to see?"

"Most of our family is in the Detroit area, so she sees all of us there. Mom would have let me know if Emily was with her, because she knew I was coming to visit her." Candace looked intently at the detective. "I'm really worried. Something has happened. You have to look for her."

"I think Emily is probably okay, but we wouldn't want anything to happen to her." Detective Perez stood up. "We'll check the local hospital and talk to the Nature Center to see if she was at work yesterday, how she seemed, whether she said where she was going after work?" Detective Perez didn't mention that they would also check the morgue. "Ryan, would you recognize the name of this new hiking trail if you heard it again?"

"I might. I don't know. There are so many trails."

"I assume she has a cell phone."

"Course. But sometimes she leaves it behind. To leave the world behind for a while, she says."

"Okay. So, she might not be able to use her phone, if she didn't take it with her or had an accident. Can you describe her for us?"

Candace paused. "I'm about 5'6" and she's a bit shorter, so probably 5'5". Her hair is medium brown, kind of wavy, about shoulder-length, and she usually wears it down. But sometimes she pulls it back when she's hiking."

"She has striking blue eyes." Ryan remembered the first time he looked into those eyes. "She's slim, athletic." The description seemed like a lame description of Emily. She was beautiful, kind, smart, hot. The cops probably weren't interested in that part of it, though.

"Any idea what she might have been wearing?"

"Jeans. Probably a long-sleeved shirt. Maybe her blue jacket, although it's been pretty warm the last couple of days."

Detective Gibson made some notes in his phone. "We'll check things out, let you know. Chances are, you'll hear something from her." He started toward the door.

"Let us know if you hear from her or think of anything else helpful. Most likely she's safe and sound somewhere."

Ryan walked to the door with the detectives and thanked them for coming. He wanted to ask them again to find Emily, but he and Candace had already said that. He hoped they would do more than just wait for her to return. He wasn't going to wait around, though. He was going to look until he found her.

Chapter 6

Detective Perez got into the passenger side of the squad car, as Detective Gibson slid his bulk behind the wheel. He turned the key and leaned back into the seat. He reached for the radio button, but changed his mind. He always listened to country music, but knew that Detective Perez did not like it. It annoyed him at times, but he tried to get along with her.

Detective Perez turned toward Detective Gibson. "So, what do you think? Is Emily really missing or just temporarily AWOL?"

"I'm guessing she's just taking some time to herself. Her boyfriend seems pretty lame to me. Dissertation and all, no real job. Is he sponging off Emily? Maybe she got tired of it. Or maybe there's something going on between the boyfriend and the sister, and Emily figured it out."

Detective Perez raised her eyebrows. "We should probably try to keep an open mind. We run into all kinds on the job and don't want to make assumptions. Don't you think? Maybe just check out the facts, look for clues."

"Right, but let's not get too touchy-feely about it. We should check back at the station to ask the Detective Sergeant what he thinks." Detective Gibson wasn't sure about this touchy-feely stuff in policing. Most people were up to something. It was best to just call them on it.

At the police station the detectives stopped by Detective Sergeant Richards' office to bring him up to date on the possibility of a missing person. It was up to him to decide which cases were most important. The Detective Sergeant was listening to someone on the phone, but waved them to the two chairs on the other side of the desk. They sat down and looked out the window behind the Detective Sergeant. A better view than the one they had from their office. A row of bushes grew along the fence that separated the station from the neighboring houses. Detective Perez thought they looked like lilac bushes. They had buds on them and would be beautiful when they were in bloom, she bet. When she had time, maybe she should plant a lilac bush or two in her yard.

After another minute, Detective Sergeant Richards hung up the phone and looked at the two detectives. He gave them his full attention while they took turns explaining what they had learned so far regarding Emily Thomas and the possibility that she was truly missing.

"Looks to me like Emily is just taking some time to herself, maybe because things aren't going so great with the boyfriend. He said they had an argument, a discussion he called it. She could have left to give him a scare, bring him around." Detective Gibson leaned back in his chair and looked at the Detective Sergeant.

Detective Perez sat up straight, sitting forward in her chair. "She may be back by tonight, but things seemed to be going well for her, so it's possible that we do have a missing-person case going."

"Well, let's not jump to conclusions or make assumptions just yet. Check the hospital and see if anyone came in without any ID. Interview the folks at the Nature Center, make sure she was at work yesterday, as Ryan seemed to think. How did she seem at work, sad, anxious, normal? See if she told a co-worker where she was going after work. It goes without saying, but check the morgue for unidentified bodies, also the nearby police stations to see if they have received any reports of accidents, or bodies. If nothing turns up, we'll give it another twelve hours. She may be back by this evening. Most so-called missing persons show up eventually. You two be the lead on this case. Check back with Candace and Ryan, if you don't hear from them, to see if there's anything new on their end. If Emily doesn't turn up by the end of the day and we have no clues about where she is, we'll need to start a search."

"Right. Will do. We'll let you know how it goes."

"Hopefully, she will be back on her own. That would be a nice ending to this case."

The detectives went back out to their patrol car. Detective Gibson slid behind the wheel again. He preferred to drive. Detective Perez rolled her eyes, as she suspected he didn't really trust women drivers. She didn't care if he drove. Sitting in the passenger seat gave her more time to think about the case.

"The hospital is on the way to the Nature Center, so let's stop there first and see what we can find out." Detective Gibson turned left and drove toward the west side of town. A sunny Friday near lunchtime brought out more traffic than they had seen lately. But the hospital wasn't far away, so it wouldn't take long for them to get there.

"Sounds good." Detective Perez leaned back in the seat, looking out the window and considering what they knew so far about Emily. Where could she be? Detective Perez was not a big nature person. She liked green grass, trees, and flowers. But more of the walk in the park variety, not hiking out in the wilderness. She couldn't imagine being stranded out in the woods all night. She shivered just to think about it. Emily sounded as if she knew how to take care of herself out there, though.

The two detectives were quiet on the drive to the hospital. They didn't have much in common, as far as they could tell, and they hadn't worked together long enough to feel totally at ease with each other.

The traffic was heavier around the hospital and the parking lot looked full. Detective Gibson pulled the patrol car into a reserved spot close to the entrance. Detective Perez rolled her eyes but didn't say anything. She wasn't averse to enjoying some perks as a cop, but she thought that she and Detective Gibson were perfectly capable of walking to get to the entrance and should leave the parking space for someone in a hurry. The detectives got out of the car and walked up the long ramp that led to the main hospital entrance.

Chapter 7

"Do you think they took us seriously? Will they look for her?" Candace picked up a photo from the table by the couch. In the photo Emily and Ryan stood in front of a rock formation that looked like a castle. "They should have asked for a picture, don't you think? Where was this picture taken anyway?"

"I think they believe she'll turn up. I don't think they'll start looking too hard right away. That was taken by someone passing by when we hiked to Castle Rock in the Pictured Rocks National Lakeshore in the UP, the Upper Peninsula. It's beautiful up there. Anyway, we can't wait for the cops. We have to make a plan of our own. I think we should go over to her apartment and see if she took her phone, or if there's any indication where she might have gone. Then we should go out and look for her until we find her."

"Good plan. I can't sit here any longer, waiting for something to happen."

Ryan paused. "What am I thinking? I forgot about Carson. He might not have had dinner last night or breakfast this morning. He'll be upset. He loves to eat and takes his meals seriously."

"Emily wouldn't have gone anywhere without feeding him. That is, if she came home last night. That cat means a lot to her."

"We can feed Carson, make sure he's okay, and look around the apartment a bit. Then we'll decide where to start looking." Ryan grabbed his jacket off the hook and headed toward the door. "Coming?" He let Candace go ahead of him and followed her out to the street.

The sun shone brightly on the brilliant green of the newly sprouted leaves on the trees. Birds called back and forth.

"The birds seem very vocal. What's the fuss?"

"Emily says they're all looking for mates. It's time for them to build nests and have families. She knows most of their calls by heart."

"That sounds like Emily. She rescued a Baltimore Oriole when she was about ten and hummed to him to keep him company." Candace laughed, and Ryan laughed with her, both thinking about the person they most wanted to find.

"We can take my car." Ryan gestured to a blue car parked on the street.

"What kind of car is this?" Candace looked the car over as she got in and fastened her seat belt.

"This is a Saab 9000," Ryan fastened his seatbelt and started up the car. "When I was ten, my Uncle Mike bought this 1986 Saab and had it restored to its original glory. It's a classic, and one of the best cars ever made. I loved this car all through my teen years, and Uncle Mike let me borrow it for the Senior Prom. When I graduated from college, he actually gave it to me. He's a great guy, my uncle."

"That was a very nice gift. Didn't any of his kids want it?"

"He never had any kids of his own. So he always took a big interest in my brother and me. My brother wasn't as interested in my uncle as I was, but Uncle Mike was good to both of us."

"He sounds like a great guy. I don't think I've come across a Saab before."

"It started out as a Swedish company that made airplanes and was always innovative and before the times. Unfortunately, it went out of business."

"Huh."

"Sorry. Don't know why I'm telling you all about my uncle and his car. I sometimes I talk a lot when I'm worried."

"It's a good distraction. Something to keep my mind off thinking up all the terrible things that might have happened."

"Don't think about that. Keep reminding yourself that we're going to find her."

Candace nodded.

Ryan pushed the speed limit as far as he felt he could to reach Emily's apartment. He parked the car on the street and unlocked the front door with the spare key Emily had given him. They climbed the stairs to Emily's apartment. Unlocking the apartment door, they stepped inside.

Ryan called, "Emily, you here?" No answer. He had hoped that they would walk in and find her here, alive and well.

Ryan looked around. "The curtains are open across the bay window. Emily would have left them open during the day to provide light for the plants that are by the windows, but she would have closed them at night. Was she here last night and left this morning, or did she not come home last night?"

"I wish I knew the answer to that."

One large room contained the kitchen/dining area, as well as the living area. In the living area, in addition to the many plants, there were a couch and two chairs, a bookcase overflowing with books, and a desk. The kitchen/dining area was small but looked clean and tidy, no dirty dishes in the sink or food left out on the counter.

They heard a thump on the kitchen counter and then a thump onto the floor. A large white cat trotted up to Ryan and rubbed his head against Ryan's legs. Ryan stroked the cat, as the cat rumbled a loud purr.

"Keeping safe on the refrigerator again, Carson? You must be hungry. Come on, let's get you some food." Carson rubbed around Ryan's legs while Ryan rinsed Carson's dish and filled it. Ryan placed the dish on the floor, and Carson began to eat. "I wish you could tell us where Emily went. Did she say anything to you?"

"If only he could talk. Emily loves this cat, but he seems like a handful sometimes. She thought he was going to be calm and friendly when she adopted him, because that's what his description said. I guess now that he feels at home, he thinks he can be wild." Candace looked around the kitchen, but there were no clues to be found there.

"He's just adventurous. Always looking for new challenges." Ryan defended Carson, though he had seen how Carson's adventures could sometimes end up breaking something.

"Why is he named Carson? I meant to ask her. After Kit Carson?"

"After Rachel Carson, you know, the environmentalist from way back."

"Figures. It suits him, though."

Ryan went over to Emily's desk and opened drawers, hoping there was something about where she might have gone. Everything was organized, bills, receipts, correspondence. He shook his head. Emily hasn't given up the paper trail yet.

"The bed is made, and everything looks in order as usual. I can't tell whether she stayed here last night or not." Candace called from the bedroom.

"Her camera isn't here. She usually takes it to work and leaves it by the door when she comes home. So it seems likely she didn't make it home after work."

"She must have had her phone with her. It's not here, as far as I can see. Wouldn't she call us if she needed help?"

"If she went hiking, she might have left the phone in the car. I've told her it's not a good idea to hike by herself without her phone, but she just smiles and says she can look after herself in the woods. I hope she's right."

"Nothing here to tell us anything about where she is now, I guess. Things seem in order, as if she just left for work."

"But didn't come back. Where could she be?" Ryan's voice choked up a bit, and he swallowed. "We should talk to someone at the Nature Center, ask if she went somewhere after work yesterday. They might tell us more than they would tell the cops."

"What about other places? We need to move faster. Time is important."

"I'll call Claire, one of the friends Emily sometimes hangs out with. They text pretty often. Claire is probably working at the bookstore." Ryan looked for the number of the bookstore and was glad when Claire answered.

"Hey, Claire, it's Ryan. Did you see Emily yesterday after work or talk to her today? I've been out of town, and I'm trying to catch up with her. She's not answering her phone."

"I worked the afternoon shift here yesterday and then went home to catch up on some things. I haven't talked to her for a couple of days. She said her sister was coming today, so maybe they're off doing something."

"Okay. That's probably it. Thanks."

Ryan disconnected. "No luck. I didn't want to tell her about Emily being missing, just yet. Maybe she's not missing and will show up. Let's just start with the Nature Center and see if they know anything that will help."

Chapter 8

Clouds drifted across the sky, at times blocking out the sun. Another day of competition between clouds and sun. Emily felt warmed from sitting in the sun, but she thought the clouds were winning the competition, blocking out the sun for longer periods of time. The increasing coolness roused her, and she considered her situation.

She tried to focus on what had happened before she ended up here. But her head still hurt, and her memory was blurry. One thing she knew for sure was that she needed to find her car. She wouldn't be able to walk home. Keys. Did she have them? She put her hands in her pockets. Her right hand closed around a set of keys. That was encouraging. Now she just had to figure out where her car might be.

Carefully, slowly, she stood and leaned against the tree. She took a step with her right food. But when she put weight on her left foot, she nearly fell, as pain shot up her leg. Had she sprained her ankle? Maybe if she rested a bit longer, the pain would subside. At least it was daylight. That made it more likely that she could find her way out. If the pain didn't ease in the next couple of hours, she would hop as far as she could, though she wasn't yet sure which direction to go.

It was important to remember what had happened. Bears. There was something about bears. Had she been attacked by a bear? She had a fond memory of finding a bear cub she rescued, but that was at least a year ago.

She had been driving along a country road on her way to meet Sara for a Sunday hike. Ahead, she spotted a large, black hump. There were no houses nearby. Why did people dump their trash wherever they felt like it?

As she drove closer, she realized it was a black bear lying by the side of the road, not moving. She pulled her car to the side of the road and got out. If the bear was injured, she wanted to get help for it, but she would need to keep her distance. She noticed movement just behind the bear and walked a few steps closer. A bear cub. It was waiting by its mother. It was early spring, so this cub must be very young. How sad. What could she do to help it? The Department of Natural Resources would know what to do.

Emily pulled her phone out of her jacket pocket and called the Nature Center to get the number for the Department of Natural Resources. Mike would be on the front desk today.

"Hey, Mike, can you get me the number for the DNR in the area? I just found a mother bear who I think was hit by a car, and her cub is beside her. It's alive, but it won't survive on its own so early in the spring."

"Poor cub. Hold on. I'll find the number and text it."

"Thanks, Mike"

A couple of minutes later, the text with the number came through on her phone, and she called it. The person who answered put her on hold, while he tried to find someone who could come out to the scene of the accident and retrieve the bear cub.

"Officer Bearman is on duty today, and he said he can get out there in half an hour or so. Keep your distance, though, until he gets there."

"Okay, thanks. I'll just wait by my car."

Emily stayed by her car, watching the cub. She did not want to get too close and scare it off. It must be hungry, but she wasn't sure what she should feed it.

Emily texted Sara to tell her why she was late to meet her and checked her email to pass the time. It was at least half an hour before the DNR officer arrived. He parked his official car ahead of Emily's car and came to stand beside her.

"I'm Officer Bearman. Mama bear got hit by a car, do you think? You sure she's dead?"

Emily looked at him curiously. Was his name, for real?

He smiled. "Yeah, that's really my name. Gets me teased a lot, but I'm fond of it."

Emily smiled. "I'm Emily. The mama bear hasn't moved, but I didn't get close enough to see if she was breathing, because I was afraid I might scare off her cub."

"I'm going to try to capture the little guy and take him to rehab. They can raise him until he's a bit bigger and can survive on his own. Once I've secured him, I'll check on the mom to see if we can save her. There aren't that many bears in the area, so we hate to lose even one."

"How will you catch the cub?"

"He's a bit young to use the tranquilizer gun, so I'll bait this live trap and place it nearby. Then we'll wait for him to take the bait and trip the door shut."

"What will you bait the trap with? I wasn't sure what a cub would eat."

"It's a mixture of formula and mushy fruit. He's probably been eating some adult food since he came out of hibernation in April. It might take a while to trap him, but hopefully he'll be tempted, especially if he hasn't eaten for a while. You can go, if you want. No need to stick around."

"I'll wait until you catch him. Just so I know he's okay."

Emily watched as the officer took out a live trap, set it a few yards away from the cub, and placed a container of food inside. The cub backed up closer to its mom as it watched.

Officer Bearman and Emily stood quietly beside her car, so they wouldn't startle the cub. After a few minutes, the cub sniffed the air and edged its way toward the trap, but didn't go inside right away.

"Where will you take him to rehab him?"

"This little guy or gal looks to be about four months old. There's a couple in southwestern Michigan who work with the SPCA to take in orphaned bear cubs. I asked the receptionist to call the rehab folks and see if they can come up and get this one. If not, I'll drive it down myself. We're lucky we have a place in the state for that. Otherwise, we'd have to try to place him in another state."

"It's great that you're willing to do that. I wasn't sure what to expect when I called, but I couldn't just leave him, or her."

"Good for you. I never pass up a chance to rescue a bear. We all felt bad about euthanizing that bear who showed up in a store parking lot. Hard to know what to do to protect the bear and protect the people."

"Do you think it will work? Will he be able to go back to the woods on his own?"

"They've had good luck with rehabbing bear cubs, and we think the cubs they've cared for did well when they were old enough to be on their own."

Emily nodded. She wondered if his last name had helped direct his line of work. "Thanks for doing that. It's good to know there's someone looking out for the little guys. And the big guys."

After a while, the cub ambled over to the trap and stepped inside to try the food mixture, and the cage door came down.

When Officer Bearman picked up the cage to put it in the vehicle, Emily peeked inside. She felt sorry for the cub, but this was his only chance of survival. "You'll be okay, little guy. You just have to grow up a bit more."

The mother bear had not reacted to what was going on, so Officer Bearman walked over to check on her. "Too bad. She's gone. I'll send someone to pick up the body."

"Would it be possible for you to let me know when the cub is released?"

"Text me your number, and I'll try to do that. Thanks for being the Good Samaritan. You could have just passed them and gone on your way."

"I was glad to help." Emily walked back to her car and texted Sara to let her know where she was. Sara said she would wait if Emily still wanted to walk. Emily said she did and would get there as quickly as she could. She got into her car, pulled out onto the highway, and waved to Officer Bearman as she left. She looked forward to telling Sara all about the cub. Sara loved bears and would appreciate the story.

Emily sighed. Why did she get caught up in all these memories? She needed to focus, to pull herself together and get moving. If a bear did have something to do with how she got here under the pine tree, she didn't yet remember what that was.

Chapter 9

The hospital was busy, as usual. Off to the right was a gift shop, and ahead of them was the front reception desk. Detective Gibson had grown up in the area. He told Detective Perez that he knew one of the gals in admitting, and they could check with her to see if there were any unusual admissions in the last 24 hours. They stopped at the reception desk and were told to go on down to admitting.

Detective Gibson nodded at a couple of people he knew, as they walked down the hall. Detective Perez was newer to the area, so did not recognize most of the people working at the hospital. She let Detective Gibson take the lead on this interview, using his familiarity with people here to get the information they needed.

At the admitting desk Detective Gibson saw that Cindy was working today. He and Cindy had dated a few times in high school, but there was no big chemistry between them. They ended up just being casual friends. They ran into each other around town occasionally and stopped for a brief chat.

Detective Gibson and Detective Perez waited in line while Cindy helped a couple of patients with some paperwork. When the couple ahead of them left, they stepped forward.

"Hey, Cindy, how's your day going?"

"Hello, Detective Gibson. Nice of you to stop by to ask about my day." She turned from her computer and smiled at him, flashing the diamond on her hand until he noticed it.

"Looks like you got lucky with some guy. Congrats." He gestured toward the ring.

"Thanks. I'd say the guy is the lucky one, though." She laughed. "What's up?"

"This is Detective Perez." Cindy and the detective acknowledged each other with a nod. Detective Gibson continued, "We're just checking on a possible missing person. Probably nothing to worry about, but we wanted to see if anyone came in, maybe to the emergency room, maybe not, name of Emily Thomas."

"Let me check. Has she had an accident or something?"

"Can't really say at this point, just need to check it out to reassure her nearest and dearest."

"Hold on. I'll look." Cindy typed into her computer while the detectives watched. People from his graduating class were dropping like flies, Detective Gibson thought, in a hurry to tie the knot. Personally, he thought there was plenty of time for that. He liked living in his own apartment and having the freedom to do whatever he wanted.

Cindy shook her head and turned back to him. "I don't see anyone by that name or anyone who came in who was unidentified."

"Okay. Thanks. If you do come across that name, call the station and ask for me, if you would."

"Sure thing." She flashed him another smile.

"Well, guess we'd better be moving along. Thanks for your help, and again, congrats. When's the wedding?"

"You're welcome. We haven't decided on a date yet. Sometime next year, I think. But weddings take a lot of planning."

Detective Gibson nodded. "Good luck with that. I'll watch for my invitation."

Cindy laughed. "A wedding reception is always a good time." In high school Detective Gibson was known as a good-time guy.

The detectives turned away and headed back down the hall and out to where the car was parked. Detective Gibson thought one of the perks of driving an official car was not having to park in a lot or pay for parking. He unlocked the door, and he and Detective Perez got in. Another car was pulling out slowly ahead of them. Detective Gibson tapped the steering wheel with his hand as he waited.

"So, doesn't look like she's had a car accident or anything. She could be lost somewhere. Maybe someone at the Nature Center will have something helpful to tell us."

"We'll check it out." The car ahead of them had finally turned. Detective Gibson pulled the police car back out into the street and took off at what Detective Perez thought was probably above the speed limit posted in the hospital area.

The Nature Center was situated on several acres at the edge of the city limits. Traffic on the road was light when the detectives got out that way. There were a few cars in the parking area and a few people walking down the trail toward the river. Detective Gibson parked near the entrance. The two detectives got out of the car and walked along the sidewalk to the door of the main building. Detective Perez noted the wildflowers planted along the walkway with tags identifying them, but did not take time to look at them. Detective Gibson opened the door, and they went inside.

An attractive woman at the counter looked up as the detectives entered and showed her their ID. The woman's name badge identified her as Sara. Sara looked a bit startled to see cops at the Nature Center.

"May I help you?" Sara searched her mind to see if she had committed any crimes, had any parking tickets. She knew that was ridiculous, but cops in uniform had that effect.

"We just have a couple of questions about an employee who works here. Emily Thomas?" Detective Perez opened up the questioning.

"She's not working today." Was Emily in trouble?

"Did she work yesterday?" Detective Perez noted the look of concern on Sara's face. "Nothing to worry about. We're just checking to be sure all is okay."

"Yes, Emily worked yesterday." Why didn't they ask Emily that question? Where was Emily? Sara frowned.

"How did Emily seem? Did she seem anxious about anything? Upset?"

"She seemed fine. We had a noisy group of middle-schoolers in the afternoon. Emily was pleased with how that went and how much the students knew. I think she felt she had done a good job with them."

"What time did she leave work?" Detective Gibson leaned on the counter. Sara took a small step back.

"She left a little early, I think, maybe about 3:30 because she had worked through her lunch hour."

"Did she say where she was going when she left? Would she have gone right home or stopped somewhere?"

Sara thought for a minute. "I think as she said goodbye, she mentioned that she was going hiking. But I was talking with a group of four who had just come in, so I wasn't paying a lot of attention."

"Any idea where she might have gone hiking?"

"Not really. Maybe one of the new trails, but she could have gone anywhere."

"Okay, thanks. If you hear from her, please ask her to call the station."

"Is Emily okay? Has something happened?"

"We think she's fine. Just making sure."

The detectives walked back out to the car. Detective Perez got into the car, thinking about what they had learned, or not learned. It sounded like Emily was fine yesterday. But how well did Sara know her? Would Emily have shared any concerns or anxieties she might have had?

"Emily was at work all day yesterday and seemed to be her usual self. Nothing out of the ordinary seems to have happened. When she left, she might have gone hiking, but Sara, the receptionist, didn't get any specific info. Maybe Emily was meeting someone. But then why didn't she contact Ryan or show up when Candace arrived this morning? Maybe things aren't as straightforward as we at first thought."

"I still think the boyfriend knows more than he is saying. He and Emily had a spat or something, and she's just giving him something to think about. I'd guess she probably met up with someone after work, maybe spent the night. Didn't want Ryan to know."

Detective Perez rolled her eyes, looking out the side window so Detective Gibson didn't notice. She decided not to comment on what he had just said. It was early in the afternoon, and Emily could still turn up.

At the station Detective Sergeant Richards was on the phone, so the detectives returned to their desks to check with the morgue and other police departments, to see if anything came up regarding Emily.

When she sensed Detective Gibson standing at her desk, Detective Perez looked up. "What did you find out?"

"Nothing to report from the other nearby police stations. No one that would match Emily's description has come in with injuries, no bodies found, no accidents."

"No new bodies at the morgue, thank goodness. Later this afternoon we should check back with Candace and Ryan. Emily knew her sister was coming today, so I'd think she'd be in touch with her."

Detective Gibson nodded and went back to his desk. "We'll give her a little more time to get in contact."

Perez felt uneasy about this case. There was no reason to think anything bad had happened to Emily. It seemed that she had a lot going right for her. A steady boyfriend, a sister she was close to, a job that she liked. So, why would she just go off and not let anyone know where she was going? They had to give it all a little more time, but Perez thought they might be organizing a search for Emily at the end of the day.

She thought about her own daughter, who had just turned thirteen. She was now coming home from school to an empty house. Detective Perez thought it was good for her daughter to have that freedom and the responsibility that went with it. But she hadn't yet adjusted to the fact that her daughter was no longer her little girl. She would become more and more independent. Of course, that was how raising a child was supposed to turn out. But that didn't make it easy to let go.

This job didn't make it easier. Seeing all the bad things that could happen to kids, she just wanted to protect her daughter and keep her safe. Detective Perez picked up the phone and called her daughter to be sure she had arrived home safely from school. Her cell phone rang, and then her daughter answered.

"Hi, Mom, don't worry, everything is fine."

"Just wondered how your day went."

"You know, just the usual. How about you?"

"Oh, you know, just the usual." They both laughed. Detective Perez had learned that it took finesse to get information out of a teenager. Timing was everything. If she didn't get a response the first time, best to let it go for now. So far, she didn't feel she had anything serious to worry about. Hopefully, it would stay that way. She had seen too many teenagers go down the wrong path.

Chapter 10

Ryan and Candace drove to the Nature Center. Sited beside the river that flowed through the downtown area farther north, it included two dark wood buildings, one small and one larger. The larger building was surrounded by a mixture of trees, both conifers and hardwoods, with a path to the side that led to the smaller building. A wooden sign saying Nature Center, with an etching of a bird and an otter, stood at the end of the parking area. An arrow pointed to a path that led to the larger of the two buildings. They walked toward the entrance, passing a garden of wildflowers.

Candace stopped to look at the identification tags by each of the flowers. "Emily planted these flowers, I'll bet."

"She did, and designed the identification tags for the flowers, too." Ryan kept walking, and Candace followed him up the walkway.

Ryan stopped when they reached the door and turned to Candace. "I don't want to get Emily in trouble. If there's really nothing to worry about, she might not want people here to think she's unreliable."

"No, she wouldn't like that."

Candace pushed open the double doors and walked in. Following her, Ryan walked up to the reception desk. "Hey, Sara, how's it going?"

"Oh, hi, Ryan. The police were just here asking about Emily. Is she okay? Has something happened to her?"

"We think everything is fine."

Sara looked curiously at Candace

"I'm her sister, Candace, visiting from Chicago." Candace held out her hand, and Sara took it.

"Chicago is a big place. Are you staying here long?"

"Just a couple of days. Did Emily go somewhere yesterday after she finished work? We haven't heard from her since she left work yesterday."

"That's concerning. I was busy with a group who had just come in. I waved when she left, about 3:30 I think it was. I wish I had said something. Maybe she would have told me where she was going. What can I do to help?"

"Do you think she went hiking after work? I know she does that sometimes, to decompress and to take photos for the nature book."

"She might have. I hope she hasn't had an accident on one of the trails or on her way home. I guess you would know if she had a car accident, though."

"We don't think she had a car accident. The cops would have checked that out. If she left here about 3:30, she would probably have gone hiking somewhere on her way home. She would want to be done hiking by dark. Do you have a map of hikes in this area?" Ryan shifted back and forth, anxiety making him want to get moving.

"Sure. Let me get one." Sara reached under the reception desk. "Oh, looks like we're out. I'll go back to the supply room and get more. Just a sec."

Waiting for Sara, Ryan distracted himself by looking at the displays in the entryway. "Look at this, a comparison of skulls. Look how large the bear skull is, compared to the lynx skull for example."

"Skulls aren't really my thing." Candace read the notices on the bulletin board. "Hey, look, there are a lot of bands playing around town. Wonder if they're any good."

"There's a lot of good music around. It's not all nature and outdoorsy stuff."

"Next time I come to visit, maybe we could check out some live music." Candace wanted to think about her next visit, with Emily safe and sound.

"Sure thing. Emily has some good ideas about music in the area."

Sara walked back into the entryway and laid a folder on the counter. "Here's a map of all the hikes in the area."

"Thanks." Ryan took the map.

"Let me know when you find her. I could help you look when I'm done here."

"Thanks, Sara. I hope we find her before then, but we'll call you if there is anything you can do. Take care."

"I'm sure you'll find her soon. Let me know she's okay."

Ryan nodded and headed out the door with Candace behind him.

"What do you think?" Candace nodded to the map Ryan was holding. "Do you know the hikes on there? Where we should start?"

Ryan scanned the map. "Looks like four hikes we could check out. These are close enough that she would be able to drive there and hike the trail on her way home. They're a place to start."

"How long would it take to hike all of them?" Candace frowned. She sometimes hiked with Emily, and hiking four trails before dark seemed impossible.

"We don't have to hike them. Her car should be in the parking area, if she was there. Still, it will take some time to drive to all four of them, as they are in different directions."

"What about the people Emily works with here? Couldn't they try some of the hiking trails? Should we tell the cops and pressure them to help?"

"Let's not pressure the cops just yet. We could go back in and talk to the Director, Brad Sykes. Emily wouldn't want him to know she's missing, but if she doesn't turn up for work tomorrow, he'll know anyway. Mike would probably help."

"Let's go ask them." Candace headed toward the entrance. Back inside the Nature Center, they saw that Sara was talking on the phone. Ryan pointed toward the hall that led to the offices with a questioning look on his face. He had gone back to talk to Brad or to find Emily before. Sara nodded. Ryan waved and walked down the hall with Candace beside him. They walked by an empty meeting room and a couple of closed doors. There were pictures on the walls of flowers, trees, and hiking trails. Ryan didn't stop to look at them.

A door on the right was open, and a middle-aged man with short, cropped hair looked up as they entered. His desk was tidy, with an open laptop and a few folders stacked beside it. A row of windows lined the back wall, giving a view of trees behind the Nature Center and a glimpse of the river glinting in the sun.

"Ryan, what can I do for you? Emily has the day off, but you must know that already."

"Hey, Brad. This is Candace, Emily's sister. Emily was supposed to meet her for lunch, but didn't show."

"Nice to meet you." Brad nodded to Candace.

"You, too."

"This is weird, I know, but Emily seems to be missing." Brad raised his eyebrows as Ryan continued. "We think she may have gotten hurt on a trail somewhere. Sara thinks Emily might have gone hiking after work yesterday. We hope to find her on one of the trails near here."

Brad frowned. "I'm sure nothing has happened to her. She is an expert hiker. Sara said a couple of cops stopped by to ask about Emily, but they didn't seem overly concerned."

"I know, but something doesn't seem right. Emily isn't answering her phone, so if she is hurt somewhere, perhaps she couldn't let us know that. There's no record that she had an accident, and we haven't been able to think of anyplace else that she would have gone. If Emily went hiking after work yesterday, we've narrowed it down to four hikes she might have taken that are close enough for her to drive there on her way home and hike the trail before dark." He pointed to the list Sarah had given them. "Candace and I can check two of them. Could you try the other two? We figure her car will be wherever she hiked, and we'll go down that trail to look for her. She might have been out somewhere all night, so it's imperative to find her ASAP."

"That doesn't sound good. I'm sure she's fine, but I wouldn't want anything to happen to her. Even the best hikers can have a mishap. Mike is working today. I'll ask him to go with me in case Emily is hurt and we need to get help."

Brad and Ryan looked at the trail maps and decided how to divide up the four locations, which ones were closest to each other. They exchanged phone numbers.

"Call if you find her car, if you find her. We'll do the same"

"One of us will find her, I'm sure of it."

Ryan and Candace drove back to his apartment. Ryan filled water bottles found a bag with snacks, and pulled a warm hoodie of Emily's out of the closet by the door. He grabbed the extra blanket from the bedroom and the first aid kit they took when going backpacking. As an education instructor, Emily had to keep her Red Cross First Aid certification current. Ryan had gone with her to get certified as well.

Candace paced by the window while he packed up. Ryan knew she was anxious, but he was anxious, too. They both needed to stay focused, to find Emily. He hoped Candace wouldn't hold them back from doing that.

"Are you okay?"

"As okay as I can be. Do you want me to carry something?" She took the blanket and the hoodie and followed Ryan out the door, down the stairs, and out to the car.

Brad walked out to the counter at the entrance. "Hey, Sara, do you know where Mike is working today? I want him to go with me to check out a couple of trails where Emily might have gone yesterday."

"I think he said he was going to repair that first bridge across the creek. Do you think Emily is in trouble?"

"I hope not, but I'm a bit worried. I'll call Mike and ask if he can go with me. I know it's still an hour before we usually close the Center, but finding Emily is the most important thing right now. You need to leave to pick up your daughter at childcare. I'll put up a sign saying that we're closing early today but will be open tomorrow as usual. We're all worried, but I'm sure we'll find her and she'll be okay."

"I could help you look. Emily might be out there somewhere, needing help."

"I know you want to help. But you need to pick up your daughter and spend time with her. We'll let you know when Emily is found. There isn't really much more you could do."

Sara nodded, started putting things away and getting out what she needed to take home.

Brad called Mike's cell phone. "Mike, I need you to come back to the Center. Ryan and Emily's sister stopped by and let us know that they haven't seen Emily today and can't reach her. They are pretty worried that something has happened, maybe she's hurt somewhere on a trail. I'm hoping you can go with me to check out a couple of trails Emily might have hiked after work."

"Sure thing. Emily is so capable out in the woods, I can't believe anything happened to her. Better to check it out for sure, though. I can finish this tomorrow. I'll grab my tools and be right there." Mike disconnected and began packing up his tools.

Brad wrote a sign and put it on the door, picked up the first aid kit and a couple of blankets they kept for emergencies. Mike filled two water bottles and grabbed some snacks from his desk drawer. Mike and Brad walked Sara to her car and waved as she drove off. They decided to take Mike's SUV. There would be more room, if they found Emily.

Chapter 11

Emily lay against the tree, listening. Every spring there were a multitude of birds in the trees singing back and forth. Birds who lived here year around, migrating birds, accidentals. They were all looking for mates. That must be stressful, she thought, having to find a suitable mate in such a short time. Having to compete with all the other birds of their kind who were looking for mates. As she listened, she tried to pick out the songs she knew. A chickadee, blue jay, woodpecker, cardinal, the regulars. She listened more carefully, maybe a tanager.

Listening to the birds brought back memories of Andy. She hadn't thought about him for a while, not since she met Ryan. He had been, she hoped he still was, a talented musician. He played guitar and violin. He used to say that listening to the birds was like listening to music. Different species represented different genres, some harsher like heavy metal or rap, some lilting like pop, some poignant like emo. She had asked him what birds sang jazz. Andy had smiled and said he didn't think birds could do jazz. Poor Andy. He was too sensitive for the music world, not confident enough to put himself forward, a bit depressed at the state of the world.

They had met when she was at a local bar with some friends and he was playing solo on his violin. When he took a break, she was at the bar getting a drink. She started up a conversation with him about his music. Emily had played violin in the high school orchestra and was impressed with Andy's talent. They started seeing each other, and then he left the area suddenly, with just a quick text to say goodbye. She was worried about him, but just wished him well. A couple of years ago she googled him, and found he had put out a record. Fortunately, when she had met Andy, she hadn't been desperate for a mate, like the birds in the spring. And then she had met Ryan.

So, what now? She wished her brain would stay focused. A trip down memory lane wasn't going to get her out of here. Wool-gathering, her grandmother called it. She was a matter-of-fact, no-nonsense woman. Emily liked her grandmother, but she was glad her mother hadn't turned out like that.

Emily stood up again and put some weight on her left foot. The pain was still sharp, but she couldn't stay here any longer. The wind had picked up a bit, rustling through the leaves and sighing in the pine trees. She picked up her camera and put it around her neck.

What she needed was a sturdy stick. Looking around near the pine tree, her pine tree she now thought of it, she saw no sticks close by that she could use. But off to her right she spotted a couple of limbs that had come down in a windstorm. One of those might work. Emily hopped and limped away from the pine tree. After a few hops she sat down to rest her ankle. Walking on her ankle hurt. Some ice would probably feel good. No chance of that out here. She got up and slowly hopped the last few steps to where the tree limbs lay.

There were two possibilities. One of the limbs was about the right length and kind of straight, but had some smaller limbs that stuck out. The other one was a bit too long and a bit bent, not as straight as she would like. She didn't have any way to cut off the limbs on the first one or to shorten the one that was too long. She tested them both out and chose the longer one.

Emily thought she could see the trail not far away. She headed in that direction. The limb helped to take some of the weight off her ankle and made traveling somewhat quicker than hopping, but it was a lot of work. She hadn't gone far when she sat down again and took a couple of deep breaths. She could do this. After a short break, she pushed herself up again and kept going.

She made it to the trail and began limping in the direction that seemed right to her. She would take her time, but she would get out of here. Even if she had to hike in the dark to make it out, she was not going to spend another night alone in the woods.

Chapter 12

Ryan stood by the car with the driver's door open, looking at the map and considering the trails they would check out.

"What now? Which one first?" Candace got into the car.

Ryan got in the car and showed her the map. "The two we have to check out are Muskrat Creek Nature Trail and Pine Lake Nature Preserve. Pine Lake is closer, so we'll go there first. Hopefully, we'll find her car in the parking area, and we'll hike that trail until we find her. It's not a long trail." Candace nodded.

When Ryan turned onto the main road, his cell phone rang. He handed it to Candace and told her his ID number. "Could you answer that? Is it Emily?" He wanted it to be her, all this just a mistake.

"It's that cop." She swiped the phone. "Hello, this is Candace. Ryan is driving."

"Hey, Candace, have you heard from Emily?" Detective Perez sounded more concerned than she had when they talked earlier in the day.

"No. We think she might have gone hiking after work, so we're checking out a couple of trails where she might have gone to see if her car is there."

"We could send a couple of guys to help do that."

"Well, thanks. We got two of the guys at the Nature Center to help check a couple of the trails. They will know the area and the trails."

"Okay. Let us know how it goes. If you don't find her, we'll pull together a bigger search. It seems we have reason to be concerned. I'll put out an alert to the area police stations." She had already talked to the Detective Sergeant, and he had agreed that she would put out the alert if there was no word about Emily by the end of the day.

"Great. Let us know if you hear anything." Candace ended the call.

"What did he say?"

"She offered to help and to pull together a bigger search if we don't find Emily. Seems like they should have been searching already. She did say she could get two guys to help us look for Emily. She also put out an alert to the police stations to be on the lookout for her"

"That sounds like progress, like they're finally taking us seriously. We'll find her. We have to." Ryan realized he kept saying that over and over. He hoped it was true. The alternative was not acceptable. What kind of boyfriend was he, if he couldn't save Emily? He pushed down on the gas pedal.

Ryan drove a few miles east of the Nature Center and turned left onto a dirt road. They passed a small cherry farm stand in front of a white house with a red barn, a few scattered houses, and a wooded area.

"Is that it?" Candace pointed to a brown, wooden sign with the name of the trail and an arrow pointing right.

"Yeah, that's it." Ryan drove down a winding, narrow road and into a small gravel parking area. Three cars were parked there, but not Emily's silver Prius. "Damn, it's not this one." He circled the car out of the parking area and drove back the way they had come.

"I wanted it to be this one. How far to the second trail?"

"I'm not sure. Could you put in the info for the Muskrat Creek Trail into the maps app? I haven't driven there from this direction before."

"Are there really muskrats in the creek?"

"Emily and I saw one once. We hiked that trail a couple of years ago. As I recall, there is a bridge over a creek."

Candace entered the name Muskrat Creek Trail into the app, and Ryan followed the directions out to the main road and back toward the west. They passed a U-pick flower farm beside a field with cows, as well as a few houses. Candace spotted the brown sign on the left side of the road, and Ryan turned into the parking area.

There were only two cars, no Prius.

"Now what?" Candace frowned.

"Call Brad and see if they've found Emily's Prius. We haven't heard from them, so probably not. But maybe they haven't checked both trails yet."

Candace chose Brad's number on her phone. It rang twice and he answered. "Candace? Any luck?"

"Hey, Brad. Nothing yet on our end. How about you?"

"No luck at Lone Oak Trail. We're almost to Kettle Lake Preserve. We'll let you know if we find her or her car. Any other thoughts?"

"No. We'll have to think of other options."

"Keep your fingers crossed. Talk soon."

Ryan and Candace sat in silence, waiting for Brad to call when he and Mike reached Kettle Lake Trail. Neither of them said anything, feeling suddenly tired and discouraged. When the call came, Brad had no good news.

Candace wiped her eyes, "Oh, my gosh, I can't bear the thought of Emily out there alone somewhere for another night. Where else could she be?"

"I don't know. I feel terrible. It's getting dark and I'm out of ideas of where to look."

They were both quiet, as they drove toward Ryan's apartment. When they reached the apartment and went inside, Candace slumped onto the couch. She felt exhausted, frustrated, worried.

"We should eat something. We have to think what to do next." Ryan pulled a frozen pizza out of the freezer and turned on the oven. When Emily came over they didn't eat frozen pizza, but he had it on hand for himself when she wasn't there. Right now he and Candace needed an easy option. When the oven was hot, he put in the pizza and set the timer. While they waited, he took two beers out of the refrigerator and handed one to Candace. They drank in silence.

The oven timer dinged, and Ryan pulled out the pizza. He put a slice on each of two plates and handed one to Candace. He sat down at the table and took a bite. He had to admit he was hungry, and eating helped him to think.

"I don't really feel like eating." Candace took a bite of pizza and chewed slowly. She took a sip of the beer Ryan had handed her.

"I know. I don't either, but maybe food will help me think. Where could Emily be?" He looked out the window. The sun was behind a cloud, but the golden light of dusk was still visible. Emily was out there somewhere. Why wasn't he smart enough to figure out where? Why hadn't she called?

Suddenly Ryan stood up. "I should have thought of that. A couple of days ago, some people came into the Nature Center talking about some blue wildflower they couldn't identify. Emily helped them look through the flower ID book, but they didn't see the flower they had observed. Emily wanted to go check it out, but hasn't had time. Maybe that's where she went to see if she could find it."

"Where was it?" Candace put aside her pizza and leaned toward him.

"That's a good question." Ryan was quiet for a few seconds. "I think it might have been the Loon Lake Trail. Because she reminded me of the time last year that we saw the family of loons out there."

Ryan looked outside. It was dusk and would be dark soon. He couldn't leave Emily out there, alone in the dark. He had to be right about Loon Lake Trail, because if that didn't work he was out of options. He didn't want to think about that. He opened a drawer in the kitchen cabinet and pulled out a flashlight.

"I'm going to drive to the Loon Lake Trail and see if Emily's car is there."

Candace stood up. "I'm coming with you."

The supplies they had taken with them before were still in the car. As he drove slowly through the city, Ryan tapped the steering wheel, impatient to get through the early evening traffic. As he turned onto the main highway, he pushed down on the gas pedal. There were a number of businesses on this road, a storage facility, boat repairs, a gas station offering pizza. He found the road he was looking for and turned left. He hoped he could remember which road turned into the parking lot. He couldn't remember if there was a sign.

Ryan saw the arrow on the turnoff sign just in time and swerved in. Candace grabbed the door to steady herself. He sped down a short gravel road to the parking area. In the parking lot of Loon Lake Trail, there was only one car. It was Emily's Prius.

"She's here somewhere." Ryan pulled his car up next to hers, and he and Candace jumped out.

Candace peered inside Emily's car. "Nothing to see."

"She must be somewhere on the trail. We'll find her." Ryan ran to the trail map posted at the trail entrance. "That's right. It's a loop trail. We could each go a different way and meet up, but I think we should stick together."

Candace nodded. She didn't want to hike alone. The woods in the sunshine seemed fine, but there were too many unexplained rustlings when things got dark. And the wind had picked up a bit. Candace hoped it didn't mean it was going to rain before they found Emily and she was safe.

Ryan and Candace took the righthand path of the trail loop and crossed an open area with some small trees and wildflowers. Emily had probably told him the names of the flowers, but he didn't remember. He tried to remember some of them when he and Emily hiked, but right now he couldn't think about flowers.

The sun was sinking lower in the sky, and dusk descended. When the trail entered the trees, the darkness deepened. Night was coming soon. Ryan pointed the flashlight down at his side as he walked, so Candace could see the trail. He knew she didn't feel all that comfortable hiking in the woods, especially at night. Even though she and Emily were close, they were different in a lot of ways.

Ryan set a brisk pace, stopping to look around, in the bushes, underneath the trees. When he heard Candace breathing heavily, he stopped for a quick break. "You okay?"

"I'm fine. Keep going. I just want to find Emily. I need to know she's okay."

Ryan nodded. "She's here and we'll find her. She's tough. It'll be okay." He set off again down the trail.

When they reached Loon Lake, he stopped again. "She might have come this way to see if the loons were here. We'd better check it out." They hurried down the short path to the lake, feeling the urgency of finding Emily as darkness closed in. The lake lapped at the shore, ruffled by a light wind.

It wouldn't be easy to hike around the lake, so Ryan thought Emily would be visible if she was here. He called her name, walked a short distance on each side of the lake until he came to dense woods. He walked back to where Candace waited, pacing back and forth.

"She's not here. Let's keep going."

They hurried back to the main trail. Ryan resisted the urge to run down it. Emily could be anywhere, and they had to look carefully so they didn't miss her. If she was injured she might not be able to call out. Every few yards Ryan stopped, and they called her name, listened. Except for some scurrying through the brush and the call of an owl, the woods were quiet. To their left they passed an unused trail.

"Emily wouldn't have taken that one. Too late in the day. She would have wanted to get home."

Candace nodded and urged Ryan forward. They continued, stopping every few yards to call Emily's name and listen for a response.

"Where could she be? Don't other people take these trails? Wouldn't someone have hiked down this trail at some point today and seen Emily? Or she would have seen them and called out?"

"Maybe. But it's the middle of the week, not yet tourist season." Ryan couldn't bring himself to consider what it might mean if Emily were unable to call out. As they continued to walk down the trail without finding Emily, he began to reconsider if she had taken the unused trail.

"You're right. Chances are, someone would have hiked this trail sometime today. Locals after work, maybe. What if Emily did take that unused trail?"

"Would she do that?"

"I think we need to look." They turned around and hiked quickly back the way they had come. When they came to the unused trail, Ryan shown the flashlight down it. "It looks like the grass is pushed down a little, like maybe someone came this way recently."

The trail was overgrown and not well-trampled, like the main trail. Tree roots bunched up through the dirt, and Candace watched her feet carefully to avoid tripping.

Farther on, Ryan tripped over a large root that snaked across the path in a sandy section of the trail. He caught himself, and looked down. "Look at that."

Candace put out her hand so as not to run into him. "What are you looking at?"

"Look at these paw prints. And the ground is stirred up. These could be bear tracks. Could a bear have attacked Emily and injured her?"

Panicked, he looked around. He spied her water bottle on the side of the trail. "That's hers. She must be nearby."

Ryan stood where he was for a minute, turning in all directions, listening, looking for signs of anything that might tell him what had happened. He started down the trail again and called Emily's name. "Emily, where are you?" He turned to Candace. "We need to check both sides of the trail. Scan the right side of the trail and look for any sign of her."

"Okay." They walked slowly down the trail, each carefully searching the area on either side of the trail.

Sitting on the ground beside the trail, Emily heard her name and looked up. It had never sounded so good to hear someone say her name. "Ryan. I'm here." Her voice sounded weak and raspy.

Ryan spied her, raced to her side, and knelt down. He wanted to put his arms around her, but he didn't know if she was injured. He gently touched her face. "Oh, Emily. I was so worried. Are you hurt?"

Emily looked at him and smiled. "I sent out wishes that you would find me. My head hurts, and I have a big bump on the back of my head. I ache all over, and I'm hungry and thirsty. I was starting to walk out, but I think I sprained my ankle, and it's slow-going."

"Okay. Don't worry. We'll get you out of here. Did you fall, do you think you bumped your head on a rock or something?" He opened the water bottle and helped her to take a few sips.

"I don't know. I don't remember anything. I think there was something about a bear. Then I woke up under a pine tree." She took a deep breath. "I don't remember where I am or how I got here. I know I was here all night. This morning I tried to leave, but I felt dizzy. Then, when I tried to stand, there was a stabbing pain in my left ankle. I found this limb and have been taking my time, limping along."

"You're just off the Loon Lake Trail. You're safe now. Do you have any wounds? Are you bleeding anywhere? Anything broken? Do you think you fell and got a concussion?" He decided not to mention the paw tracks that he and Candace had seen. Plenty of time later to talk about that.

"I don't know. I don't think I have any wounds, just the bump on my head and a sprained ankle."

Candace knelt on Emily's other side. She blinked away tears and put an arm around Emily's shoulders. "We finally found you. Are you okay?"

"I am now." Emily began to cry, just like when she was little and her big sister comforted her.

"Hush. We'll get you out of here soon." Candace draped the blanket she had been carrying over Emily and tucked it around her. "You'll be right as rain, whatever that means."

Emily tried to smile. Candace was good in a crisis.

Ryan told the person who answered his 911 call about Emily's possible injuries, the need for an EMT, and the trail they were on. "When you get to the trail entrance, take the left side. It's a loop trail, and we are more than halfway around it."

Ryan looked at Emily, trying not to show how concerned he was about how long it might take to get the EMTs out here. Should he try to carry her out? He thought a medical person should check to determine what injuries she had, before she was moved. And she couldn't walk on that ankle. He felt frustrated that he couldn't make everything better.

"I'd better call Brad and Mike, let them know we found you."

"What do they have to do with it?" Emily looked at Ryan.

"I'll explain it all later. They're helping us to look for you."

Ryan walked a few feet away from Emily and called Brad. He answered immediately.

"How is she? Is she injured? Do you know how she ended up there?"

"She's okay, has a bump on her head and probably a sprained ankle. Tired and hungry. I called 911, since I don't think she can walk out of here. I don't know how bad her injuries are."

"Right. We're just glad you found her. Tell her not to worry about work. We'll take care of things until she recovers. Glad she's safe."

Ryan knew that keeping Emily home and quiet would be a struggle. She would think she needed to be at work. First things first. Get her checked out at the hospital to make sure she had no serious injuries.

Emily closed her eyes, as Candace and Ryan each held her hand, trying to warm her up. Candace started singing songs that she and Emily had learned at camp when they were growing up. Emily felt too weak to join in, but hummed along, soothed by the familiarity of singing with Candace. They had won a talent show once in elementary school when they sang a duet.

After a short while, Ryan left Candace to take care of Emily and walked to where the unused trail met the main trail. He paced up and down, wishing that the EMTs would arrive. When he spied them hustling along the trail with a folded gurney, Ryan over to the middle of the trail and waved the flashlight to make sure they would see him.

"We're here." Ryan called out, relieved. He guided them back to where Candace and Emily waited.

The two EMTs efficiently checked Emily's pulse, temperature, and blood pressure, and looked for injuries. "Looks like a big knot on the back of your head. Did you take a fall?"

"I don't know. I just know my head hurts."

"She's been here since yesterday evening. She doesn't remember if she fell, or how she got off the trail."

The EMT nodded. "Some swelling of the ankle. Probably sprained. Otherwise, just bruises and scrapes, I think. A bit dehydrated. It's okay to drink some water."

"So, she's mostly okay?"

"They'll check her over more carefully when we get her to the hospital. They'll may want to keep her overnight. She might have been concussed. She needs some food and water. And plenty of rest, I'd guess."

Ryan handed Emily the water bottle.

"I just want to go home." Emily teared up again.

"I know, but we should go to the hospital. It's best to be careful, be sure all is okay."

"What about Carson?" Emily looked at Ryan.

"We fed him earlier, and we'll bring him back to stay at my place tonight."

Ryan and Candace followed the EMTs who carried Emily back down the trail to the parking lot. Candace took Emily's keys and drove her car behind the ambulance, while Ryan followed in his car. The ambulance kept up a steady speed but did not use its siren, as Emily's injuries were not life-threatening. One of the EMTs sat in the back beside her. Emily closed her eyes, glad to have other people taking care of things. Before they arrived at the hospital, she was asleep.

Chapter 13

At the hospital the EMTs wheeled Emily into the emergency room and transferred her to a wheelchair. Ryan pushed the wheelchair into the registration line, and the three of them waited for Emily to be checked in. The woman standing ahead of them, holding a small child in her arms, signed the necessary forms and went to sit in the waiting area. Candace arrived and handed Emily the purse that she had brought in from Emily's car. The nurse at reception asked Emily some questions and copied her insurance information.

Having seen Emily checked in, the EMTs left her to the care of Ryan and Candace. Ryan wheeled Emily over to the waiting area, and the three of them waited for a doctor to be available. Ryan held Emily's hand. He could tell she was in pain, but she didn't say anything. After a while she closed her eyes, and he thought maybe she had gone to sleep.

Candace shifted impatiently, worried about Emily and frustrated at how slowly the ER seemed to move through all the patients. A man in a chair across from them grimaced and let out a moan from time to time. He seemed to be alone, and Candace felt sorry for him. Finally, a nurse called Emily's name and showed them to a cubicle, where they waited again for a doctor to arrive.

A tall woman in a white coat entered the cubicle, nodded to Ryan and Candace, then looked at Emily. "Hi, I'm Dr.

Warner. How did you get a bump on the head and maybe a sprained ankle?"

Emily sighed. "I don't know. I was hiking, and then I found myself lying under a pine tree with a bump on my head. When I tried to stand up, I felt a sharp pain in my left ankle and it was hard to walk on it."

"Did you fall? Hit your head on a rock, maybe?"

Emily shrugged. "I don't really remember what happened." She blinked away tears, feeling helpless and ridiculous. She just wanted to go home and forget all this.

"Sounds like you are having some trouble remembering. Let me examine you and see what the damages are." She turned to Ryan and Candace. "Please wait out there while I examine Emily. We'll call you back in when I'm done checking her out."

Ryan squeezed Emily's hand, and he and Candace gave her a gentle hug. She seemed fragile. The two of them stepped outside the cubicle and sat down to wait.

Dr. Warner shined her penlight into Emily's eyes, gently touched the bump on her head, and moved her legs and arms to check for broken bones.

"Seems like you may have had a concussion, since you're having trouble remembering what happened. Your ankle is swollen, so it's probably sprained. What about other symptoms? Dizziness? Nausea? Blurry vision? Confusion?"

"All of the above except blurred vision. Are those signs of a concussion?"

"Yes. Given your problem with remembering, I'd guess you were out for a few seconds, anyway. We don't know how long you were out, but your symptoms are probably related to a concussion. Most concussions resolve themselves in seven to fourteen days. The main thing is to take it easy and get plenty of rest. No sports or strenuous physical activity. For the sprain, ice the ankle for a day or two to bring down the swelling, and go easy on it until it has healed. Take acetaminophen for pain, if you need it. Do you have any questions?"

"Do you think I will remember what happened?"

"Probably, but not necessarily. The main thing is not to dwell on remembering, just give your brain some time to heal. We'd like to keep you overnight to be sure you're okay. We'll see how you're feeling tomorrow, but I expect you'll feel much better and be ready to go home."

"I'd rather go home now."

"I understand, but with a concussion it's best to be cautious. Especially since we don't know what happened."

The doctor came out and motioned Ryan and Candace to come in. "Relax," she said, seeing their worried faces. "Looks like Emily had a concussion. A bit more serious than a mild one, as she might have been out for a few seconds. But with rest for a few days, she should feel okay. I gave her something for the pain. There's a bump on the back of her head. I'd say she fell and hit her head on something. Were there rocks where she fell?"

Ryan shrugged. "I think there are some rocks along the trail. The trail was pretty rough, not often used. A lot of tree roots across it." He looked at Candace.

"I didn't really see rocks, but I did have to watch my feet to keep from tripping on those tree roots."

The doctor looked at both of them intently. Then she turned to Emily. "The bump on your head should heal itself. You need fluids, since you were out in the cold and are a bit dehydrated. Mainly, you need rest."

"Emily mentioned a bear. Could she have been attacked? Are there other injuries?" Ryan put his hand on Emily's shoulder and looked at the doctor.

"Just bruising, probably from when she fell. No wounds that might have been caused by a bear attack."

"That's a relief."

"We think Emily should stay overnight for observation. She's not keen on the idea."

"I just want to go home." Emily looked at Ryan and Candace, wanting them to take her home.

Candace patted Emily's shoulder. "I know. I don't blame you, but I think it's a good idea to be sure all is okay. You don't know exactly what happened to you, and you don't want complications from the concussion."

"Candace is right." Ryan kissed her forehead. "We'll come and take you home tomorrow."

Emily gave a big sigh, but did not continue to object.

Ryan walked over to the window and called Detective Perez. He left a message to let her know they had found Emily and what the doctor had said about her injuries. Ryan and Candace followed Emily to the second floor and watched as she was settled into bed. She seemed too tired to talk, so they just sat with her until she fell asleep.

Ryan and Candace left the hospital and walked to the parking lot.

"I think you should stay at my place tonight. You shouldn't be alone."

Candace nodded. "It's been a strange day. I wish we could take Emily home."

"Me, too. Do you think you could drive Emily's car back to her apartment? I'll follow you and pick you up there."

"I think so." Candace realized she was trembling from the shock of Emily being missing and then finding her injured on the trail. She took a couple of deep breaths and got into Emily's car. Ryan drove carefully, making sure Candace was keeping up behind him.

At Emily's apartment they stopped to pick up Carson and pack up some food and toys for him. Carson was clearly glad to see them and snuggled up to Candace, as she carried him to the car. At his apartment Ryan grabbed Candace's travel bag from her car, which was still parked on the street.

He fed Carson and made up a bed on the couch for Candace. "Will you be all right out here? Need anything?"

"I'm fine. Thanks."

Ryan went into the bedroom and lay on his bed, looking up at the ceiling. Life was short. You could lose someone you cared about so easily.

Candace lay down on the couch. Carson draped himself across her legs, always the attentive host. She called Josh. He had just finished at the restaurant and was on his way home.

"Hey, didn't expect to hear from you. Thought you and Emily would be out late partying."

Hearing Josh's voice, Candace choked back tears, and didn't speak for a few seconds. "No, that didn't happen."

"What's wrong. You okay?"

Candace told him about Emily being missing and finding her alone and injured in the woods.

"Sounds tough. But you and Ryan did well. You found her. It'll all be okay."

"You're right. The worst is over. Miss you. I'll be back in a couple of days."

"Miss you, too. Get some sleep. Talk to you tomorrow."

Candace disconnected and closed her eyes.

Chapter 14

Saturday

When Ryan and Candace arrived at the hospital the next morning, Detective Perez and Detective Gibson were already there. Detective Gibson stood by the door while Detective Perez sat in a chair by the bed talking quietly to Emily. Emily looked tired, but she was sitting up. Candace squeezed her hand, while Ryan leaned over and kissed her cheek. They both stood back to give Emily space to talk with Perez.

"You think you saw a bear, and then you woke up in a depression under a pine tree? And you don't remember how you got there."

Emily shook her head slowly. "I wish I could remember. It seems important, but it's all just a blur right now."

"Ryan and Candace thought they saw bear paw prints on the trail near where you were found, but you don't have injuries consistent with a bear attack. The doctor says you have a bump on the back of your head. Maybe you panicked when you saw the bear and fell?"

Emily shook her head. "None of it makes any sense to me. I was just taking a hike and photographing some flowers I hadn't seen before. When I saw the bear, I didn't feel scared, not really. I think I started to back up slowly, as I was told would be the right thing to do."

"The Doctor says you've had a concussion, so you need to rest. Maybe you'll remember more about what happened when you are better rested. You have my card from our conversation with Ryan, if anything comes up. Otherwise, I think this is a good ending to what could have been much worse."

Detective Perez stood up, said goodbye, and left with Detective Gibson.

"Take me home, Ryan. I need to get out of here. Did you pick up Carson last night? Was he okay?"

"If the Doctor says it's safe for you to leave, I'll take you to my apartment and take good care of you. Carson is fine. He sends his love and hopes you will be home soon."

"Can you stay in town, Candace? I feel badly that you came all this way and now I can't show you the sights or do anything fun with you."

"Well, I am going to stick around for a couple of days until you're feeling better. I can stay at your place, and you can stay at Ryan's. We're going to look after you."

"Thanks. I'm so glad you're here." Emily leaned back and closed her eyes. Ryan and Candace sat quietly holding her hands, thinking about what could have happened on the trail and whether Emily would remember it.

When the doctor entered the room, Ryan and Candace stood up. The doctor went over to Emily's bed. "How are you feeling this morning?"

"Better. Still tired. I wish I could remember more about what happened. Will my memory come back?"

"Try not to worry about remembering. Chances are the memories will return when you've had some time to rest. That's most important: rest and relaxation, without stress, to give your brain time to recover."

"But can I go home?" Emily's eyes teared up.

"I don't see why not, as long as someone will be with you for a couple of days. Just to be sure there are no complications. I expect you'll be fine in a couple of days. No hard athletics, though. Take it easy."

"I'll take her to my apartment, so she doesn't have to walk up the stairs with a sprained ankle. I'm home working most of the time and will make sure she rests and gets better." Ryan smiled at Emily, and she nodded her thanks.

"And I plan to stick around until I know she's okay." Candace squeezed her sister's hand.

"All right then. I'll have the nurse get your discharge papers ready and give you a prescription for a stronger acetaminophen. Make an appointment with your regular doctor in a couple of days, just to be sure everything is going okay."

Candace helped Emily get dressed and gather up the few things she had with her at the hospital. About thirty minutes later, the nurse arrived with discharge papers for Emily to sign. Ryan pushed her in a wheelchair out to the parking lot and carefully helped her into the car, trying not to hurt her head or her ankle.

"Just drop me off at Emily's apartment. I need some sleep, and your apartment will be too crowded for the three of us. I'll come over later and get my stuff."

"Okay. Use anything you need in the apartment. Do you have the key?" Candace shook her head. Emily felt in her jacket pocket and handed her the key.

"So sorry you came all this way just to look after me."

"Just wish you didn't have to get a concussion before I got here. Get some rest, and I'll see you this afternoon." Candace leaned into the car and hugged Emily. She walked up the steps and waved as she let herself in.

At Ryan's apartment building, three steps led up to the porch that stretched across the front. Ryan opened the door to his apartment and held Emily's arm as she hopped carefully up the steps and went inside.

Carson ran to her, purring loudly, and she scooped him up. "Hey, Carson. I'm glad to see you." She rubbed under his chin. "After I take a shower, I think I'll just lie on the couch for a while, if I won't be in the way. I don't feel like doing much, but I hate lying in bed all day."

"Course. Whatever you want. Do you want to eat something? Did they feed you at the hospital?"

"I couldn't eat much of what they gave me, so I guess I am a bit hungry."

"Toast? Eggs? Pancakes?"

"Toast with peanut butter sounds good. And coffee."

After Emily showered, Ryan made sure she was comfortable on the couch with a pillow to prop up her ankle and a bag of ice for it. He went into the kitchen and made toast and coffee. She took the toast and ate slowly. Ryan didn't try to get Emily to talk. He could tell that she was tired.

After eating, Emily dozed off, with Carson laying on her feet. Ryan sat for a while watching her, still worried. Finally, he stood up, went to his desk, and tried to get some work done. He stared out the window. What had happened on Loon Lake Trail? He didn't get much work done.

Later that afternoon Candace arrived with groceries. Emily was sitting up, listening to music. She smiled when she saw the groceries. Candace always took care of things.

"Did you get some sleep?" Candace set the groceries on the kitchen table.

"Yes. What have you been doing? I'm sorry that I haven't shown you much of a good time since you got here."

Candace laughed. "Well, it's been interesting, anyway. I'm so sorry you hit your head. Does it feel any better?"

"The pain meds they gave me help a lot. I feel kind of groggy, though, which I don't like." Emily frowned. "I still don't remember what happened after I saw the bear. But my head hurts when I try to remember."

"Just don't think about it until you feel better. You'll remember when you're ready. That's what the doctor said."

"You're probably right. What kind of groceries did you bring with you?"

"I picked up some things to make dinner. Salad makings, tofu, vegetables, and ice cream."

"Sounds great. I should be cooking for you, though."

"I'll make you cook when you come to visit me in Chicago." Candace noticed Ryan's grimace when she mentioned tofu. "It's really good. That guy I've been seeing, Josh, is the chef at this new restaurant. He taught me how to make it."

Emily turned to Ryan. "Sounds serious. She told us his name and what he does for a living. Maybe he's a keeper."

"Early days, but seems promising." Candace gave her a playful poke in the arm and changed the subject. "Did Ryan tell you about the contemporary art exhibit?"

"No, not yet, what is it?"

"Contemporary art by women artists. Paintings not seen very often in the past. I'll email you the brochure. You two should come and see it."

"Sounds good. Will we get to meet Josh, the nice chef?"

Candace smiled. "Maybe."

"I'm sure the tofu will be great. Nice of you to bring stuff. What can I do to help?" Ryan took the bag from Candace. He could usually eat most anything, if he was really hungry.

"Come on into the kitchen, and I'll put you to work."

Ryan put on another record and went into the kitchen to chop vegetables. He and Candace didn't try to make conversation, just listened to music and cooked. When dinner was ready, Ryan helped Emily to the table.

"Hey, this is actually pretty good." Ryan looked at the tofu in surprise. "We'll have to check out this chef."

Candace laughed. "Told you it would be delicious."

After dinner Ryan cleared the table while Candace dished up three bowls of ice cream. When she started to help Ryan with the dishes, he gestured for her to join Emily at the table.

"I love this coconut ice cream. But I feel weird being waited on like this."

"Enjoy it while you can. More ice cream?" Emily shook her head, and Candace put the ice cream into the freezer.

Ryan wiped off the counter and sat down at the table. He looked at Candace. "So, what were you two like growing up together? My brother and I were farther apart in age than you are. We played together some, but fought a lot, too." Ryan took a bite of ice cream.

"Emily would probably say I was a bit bossy, but I'd say I showed good leadership skills."

"Bossy probably describes it." Emily paused. "But I always thought you were so cool, you know."

"You were right about that." They both laughed. "I think we got along pretty well, though. We had a few fights, but we played together a lot, and when we had friends over, all of us would make up some game together."

"That's true. As siblings go, I think we got along. Still do."

After Candace left, Ryan and Emily started watching part of a mystery series they had been following. Carson sat on Ryan's lap, looking at the television as if he were watching the show with them.

"So, Candace doesn't have a steady guy in her life?"

"No. She was in a serious relationship in high school, but they went to different universities and their relationship cooled. Dad died suddenly when she was a sophomore in high school. She dated at university, but after Dad died, she seemed focused on her career and having a good time."

"She and your dad were close?" Ryan rubbed Carson's head and under his chin.

"Very. He and I got along okay, but he and Candace just seemed to be in sync about things. Maybe she's afraid to care too much about someone, since people can die suddenly."

Ryan wondered if Emily felt that way as well, but decided it was better not to suggest that. "Maybe this chef will turn out to last. He makes good tofu, and that's an achievement."

Emily laughed. She looked at the TV screen and realized she hadn't really been following what was happening on the show for the past several minutes.

A few minutes later Ryan noticed Emily's eyes were closed. "Shall I turn this off? We can watch it later."

"My head is starting to hurt."

"Come to bed. You'll feel better tomorrow."

"You're coming with me?" Emily sat up and carefully put her feet on the floor.

"Definitely. I missed you last night." Ryan put his arm around her and helped her to stand without putting weight on her left foot. She leaned against him and sighed. She hated being so helpless, but it felt great to have Ryan's arm around her. Safe and warm.

Emily put on her pajamas and crawled into bed. She snuggled close to Ryan, and he held her until he fell asleep. His regular, relaxed breathing soothed her, and finally she fell asleep as well.

Later in the night she awoke from a dream. An unknown creature chased her through the woods, and she was trying to run away with a broken leg. She snuggled closer to Ryan and tried to get comfortable without lying on the bump on her head. What had happened out in the woods? She would not feel okay until she figured that out and dealt with it, whatever it was. And what would she do with this sprained ankle? She certainly couldn't take people on hikes. Hopefully, her ankle would heal soon. Lying around was not an appealing idea.

Chapter 15

Sunday

The following day Emily got out of bed and took a shower. She washed her hair gingerly to avoid the bump on her head. She dressed in comfortable clothes and limped out to the kitchen, where Ryan was making coffee.

"Thought you would sleep in longer. You okay? Sit down. How's your ankle?"

"I slept okay for a while, then had a hard time finding a comfortable position for my head. My ankle still hurts. But don't worry. I'm happy to be here and not lying underneath that pine tree, although it was a very nice tree. Comforting to smell fresh coffee."

Ryan poured a cup and handed it to her. "Toast? Anything else?"

"Toast sounds good right now."

Ryan made toast for both of them and poured himself a cup of coffee. He sat at the table with Emily, pleased that she was here again. "You should probably rest today. Candace will be over later."

"Yeah, I don't feel like doing much. I still feel sore all over and tired."

Emily lay on the couch with Carson and read a book she had taken out from the library about the origin of the first people in the Americas. It was interesting but required her concentration, so she laid it aside and took a nap. When she woke, she saw that Ryan was working at his desk. She was pleased that her being here did not distract him so much that he couldn't work.

Ryan looked over and saw that she was watching him. "What is it?"

"Just glad you're able to work. I was afraid my being here would get in your way and you wouldn't get anything done."

"Won't happen. Carson is sure sticking close to you since you got back. He's usually planning his next athletic stunt."

"He's a good caregiver. When did Candace say she was coming over?"

"I think she said she was doing some shopping this morning and then would be over to take you to the beach to enjoy the sun, if you want to do that,"

"That sounds great. You know, I've been thinking. What do you think about taking a trip to Hawaii?"

"I've always wanted to go to Hawaii. What made you think about that?"

"We don't take enough vacations. I know we couldn't go right away. We couldn't afford it. But I thought maybe we could start thinking about it, make some plans."

"Sure. I'm in."

When Candace arrived, Emily was dressed in layers. She knew it was too cold to go swimming, but they could sit on the beach in the sun. Candace was prepared with a beach blanket and a bag with snacks and water. "I thought about bringing beach towels, but I'm pretty sure the water is still too cold even for wading."

"The weather has been unseasonably warm, but the water temperature probably isn't above 50 degrees, if that. After enduring the cold while lying outside for a night, the thought of

Lake Michigan water makes me shiver. I'll take the warmth of the sun."

Candace drove her car, while Emily directed her to the downtown parking lot across from the beach. She parked the car, and they walked through the tunnel under the waterfront road, which led to the marina and the beach.

"Hey, look at that." Candace stopped and looked at the mural painted along the walls of the tunnel. "Who did these? They're beautiful, and fun."

"Anishinaabe artists. The city contracts with artists to mount their art on the tunnel walls."

"Great idea." Candace gazed at the painting as they walked through the tunnel. "I like that canoe with the people in it. It has a feeling of movement."

She stopped again farther down. "Look at that wolf's head. And those eyes. It feels like it's looking right at me."

"That's one of my favorites. It would be interesting to meet a wolf in the wild."

"If you say so."

At the end of the tunnel sat a man strumming a guitar and singing. Candace fished a couple of dollars out of her pocket and laid them in the guitar case. The man nodded.

A few people were enjoying the spring sunshine on the beach, but it wasn't crowded. Candace spread out the blanket and set their water within reach. They sat down and watched the waves lapping the shore.

"Any luck with remembering what happened out there in the woods?"

Emily sighed and shook her head slowly. "Not much yet."

"Hey, don't worry. It will come back to you."

They lay back on the beach blanket and closed their eyes.

After a few minutes Candace sat up and looked at Emily. "You seem to have a thing with bears. Didn't you say you rescued a bear cub a while ago?"

Emily sat up slowly. Changes in position still affected her balance a bit. "It was several months ago. It was weird, when I was stuck in the woods I kept remembering random things. You know how they say when you face death, your life flashes before you? I knew I wasn't facing death or anything like that, but memories kept popping up somehow. So, I was thinking about the bear cub when I was lying out there in the woods. The cub was so cute and seemed so vulnerable beside its dead mother. I wanted to do something for it."

"What happened to it?"

"The DNR man, Mr. Bearman — yeah, I know, but it's his real name — took the cub to a rehab place for bears somewhere in southwest Michigan. I called him a few weeks later to check on the little guy. He told me the bear was doing well, not so little anymore, and they planned to try to release him. But I never heard where they let him go. Mr. Bearman said they usually don't give you that information, because they don't want people to get worried about bears in their area."

"Huh. It was nice of you to save the cub. And that guy sounds like a real bear lover."

"Yes, he was."

"You thinking about Dad? It's been a long time since he died, but I still miss him."

"Me, too. This year I've been thinking about him more than usual. I often spend a quiet moment remembering him. But I've been thinking about the fact that he will never know I got the job at the Nature Center. He will never meet Ryan, or Carson. If I have kids, they won't know their grandfather."

"I think about such things, too. But then I comfort myself with the thought that he knows we're doing well, which makes me feel better. How do you think Mom is doing? She always seems so serene about life."

"That's just how Mom is. She still grieves at times. I can tell when she gets more quiet than usual and spends time by herself. But she has always tried to keep up a good front for you and me."

"She kept us all together after Dad died."

"She did, and she found a way to move on, even be happy, I think." Emily paused, not sure if she should bring this up. "What would you think if she found some guy that she liked, that she wanted to live with or something?"

Candace looked surprised. "Do you think she could find anyone as great as Dad?"

"No, probably not, but maybe someone she could share her life with. I don't want her to always have to be alone."

"That's true. We'll take that if it comes, I guess."

Emily nodded. She had a feeling it might happen soon. Their mom had been a bit mysterious, even a bit evasive, one time recently when Emily had asked her what she was going to do on the weekend. Maybe she should let her mom know that if she did meet someone, it would be okay with her.

"So, how are things going with Ryan?"

"Great. We seldom argue, and we enjoy doing things together. He's kind and thoughtful most of the time."

"Is that it? Sounds a bit ho-hum."

Emily laughed. "Okay, the sex is great, too."

"That's more like it."

They both sat up and looked out at the water. A couple of families were packing up blankets and beach toys. The kids looked tired but happy. One of the dads picked up a toddler, who rested his head on his dad's shoulder.

"What about your chef guy?"

"He's not mine, not exactly." Candace smiled. Maybe he was. She and Josh hadn't really talked about what kind of relationship they had. It just seemed to develop without the need to discuss it.

"Maybe not yet. What's he like? Is he from Chicago? Has he always been a chef? How did you meet him?"

"He grew up in Chicago, went to college to become a CPA to help out his parents. He always liked to cook and often made dinner for friends. So, he went to chef school, did an internship in New York City with a French chef. He came back to Chicago and has worked in a few restaurants. Then a guy he knew was opening this new restaurant and asked him to be the head chef. We met at the restaurant, actually. He came out to talk with the customers, to ask how we liked what we'd ordered. We got into a great discussion about food. Things moved on from there."

"So, you clicked right away, I guess."

"Being a chef is really hard work, so he's really fit. He's not the stereotypical plump chef."

"Ah. It's his body you're really after."

"Well, partly." She laughed.

Candace nudged Emily, nodding toward the trees bordering the sidewalk. "You see that guy walking toward the marina by himself, over there?"

"The one in the black tee?"

"Yes, that one."

"What about him?"

"He was leaning against that large tree for a while. Whenever I looked at him, he seemed to be staring at us. But when he saw me looking at him, he looked away."

"Maybe he was watching you because you're so good-looking."

"Oh, right." Candace rolled her eyes. "I don't think so."

"No, really. Why else would he be watching us? Or maybe he was looking at something else."

"Well, maybe he was looking at you. You're beautiful."

"No, you've always been the stunner in the family. It's fine with me."

"Okay. We're both beautiful then."

They both laughed. "We should head back."

They packed up their things. Candace insisted on carrying almost everything, as she was worried that Emily wasn't taking it easy enough since the concussion. They walked through the tunnel under the road back to their car in the parking lot. Again, Candace stopped every few feet to look at the paintings on the tunnel walls.

As they approached their car, Candace noted that the guy in the black tee was leaning against a vehicle not far from theirs, looking at his phone. He did not look up as they passed him. He may not have been watching them at all, just looking around at the beach.

Emily and Candace got back to Ryan's apartment late in the afternoon, tired and relaxed. He told them he had gotten a lot done on his dissertation. They congratulated him and put their beach gear away.

"Time for dinner. You hungry? We have stuff to make a salad, burritos with guacamole and corn chips. And there's still ice cream."

"Sounds good. I'll make the salad." Candace went into the kitchen, pulled the ingredients out of the refrigerator, and began tearing lettuce and chopping vegetables into a bowl.

Emily sat at the kitchen table and talked to Candace and Ryan as they prepared dinner. They wouldn't let her help. She thought that was silly, but didn't say so. During dinner they talked about ordinary things, plans for the summer, what they were doing at work, how members of their family were doing.

"I hate to say it, but I think I need to drive back to Chicago tomorrow. We have that special exhibit opening the day after tomorrow that I'm needed for. Also, Mom seems to have picked up that something is amiss. I think we should her something. What do you think?"

"If she asks, tell her I had an accident on the trail, fell and hurt my head, and Ryan is taking care of me while I recover. Tell her I'm fine. I'll call her when I feel better."

"Okay. I hate to leave you. I can come back. You'll let me know if you need anything?"

"I'm feeling much better. It's been great having you here. Wish it had been more fun for you. Next time I'll show you a really great time, I promise."

"Ryan and I decided that we should check out the music scene next time I come."

"Okay. We can do that." Emily smiled, pleased that Candace and Ryan had made plans together.

Ryan and Emily walked Candace out to the porch. They waved as Candace got into her car and drove away.

Emily laid her head on a pillow and put her feet on Ryan's legs, so they could share the couch. Carson jumped up and claimed a space beside them.

"Ryan, I feel like an idiot. I haven't even asked you about your dissertation meeting. How did the meeting go? Did they think you were on the right track? Are you feeling better about it?"

"No problem about not asking. We've had other things to worry about. The meeting with my advisors went well. That one guy is still a bit full of himself, giving me more advice than I would like, but mostly the three of them think I'm on the right track. They encouraged me to get it done. I've made some progress in the last couple of days, so I think it's okay."

"Well, I'm feeling better, so you don't have to babysit me. You can work on the dissertation as much as you want. What did they think about the unsung-heroes part? You were concerned they wouldn't think it was important."

"They had some questions about how I would determine who the unsung heroes were, but I think I convinced them by giving examples. Like in the Civil Rights Movement, there were heroes that everyone knew about, such as MLK Rosa Parks, Medgar Evers, Harriet Tubman. But real change came about because of all the regular people who came out to protest or demonstrate, to risk being beaten or arrested by racists. Who didn't back down until they got the powers that be to change the laws."

"Sounds like you presented a good case for it." She smiled at him. "What did they think about the part regarding what makes some people choose to be heroic, while others choose not to be?"

"They convinced me to leave that to the psychologists. They didn't think it had a place in my dissertation. I've often wondered why some people choose to do daring things to help others, but I agree with the committee that I need to stay more narrowly focused and not include extra stuff."

"Makes sense. Did you have time to get together with anyone? Your text said you were out with friends."

"I stayed with Chris. He and I hung out downtown for a while that first evening. He's doing okay and still seeing Val."

"That's good. I like her."

"I do miss some of the people we know down there, some of the friends we hung out with."

"Me, too. We should both go down and spend some time with them. Change of subject. Here's the thing. I want to hike the Loon Lake Trail with you, to try and remember what happened that day on the trail. And then I want to move back to my apartment for a couple of days."

"That doesn't seem like a good idea. You're supposed to be resting, taking it easy. How are you going to get up and down those stairs?"

"I know I need to rest, and I will. But I need to feel okay again about being in the woods, about being at my apartment. I've lost the feeling of safety that I can hike alone, or even be alone. I need to reclaim myself and not feel like I have to be with someone to be safe."

"Don't you think that will come in time?"

"I don't know, but I need to reclaim it now."

Ryan sighed. "If that's what you need to do, I won't try to talk you out of it. How long do you intend to stay by yourself? Can I come over and spend the night?"

"Of course, you can spend the night. It won't be any different than it has always been. I just won't be here all the time, and you won't have to wait on me."

"When you are in your apartment, you'll lock the door?"

"I always lock the door. Where I grew up, everyone locked their doors. I think most people who live here do, too."

"You're right, I've been worried about you since you went missing, so I'm fussing too much. You're not supposed to drive for a few days. I can drive you wherever you need to go."

"That'll be great, but if you have things to do, I can take a bus or get a ride with someone. I don't want you to have to chauffeur me all over."

"Like I wouldn't want to do that. Course I'm happy to drive you."

"Okay. That would be great. I don't think I'll be going places much for a while anyway."

"Brad said you should take off whatever time you need to heal. They can manage for a while without you."

"I don't want to be gone too long. They might decide they don't need me after all. And Mike and I need to get that book finished."

"I don't think there's any chance they would decide they can do without you. And you can work on the book at home, maybe have more time to think about it."

"You're right. Maybe I can get my part mostly done, while I'm home."

Chapter 16

Monday

The next morning Emily took a long shower, got dressed, and packed her backpack. She heard Ryan in the kitchen making coffee. She walked in, put her arms around him and kissed him. "Good morning."

"Good morning. You sure about moving back? You know you can stay here as long as you want." Ryan poured them each a cup of coffee.

"I know, and you're a great nurse." She smiled. She was reluctant to leave the safety and comfort of staying with Ryan. But she needed to regain her sense of control over her life and didn't want to worry him more.

Ryan laughed. "If the dissertation is a failure, I guess I could try nursing."

"The patients would love you."

"Toast? Eggs? Fruit? You should eat breakfast."

"All that sounds good. I'm hungry. Wish it was strawberry season."

"It will be soon. For now, there are berries from the Co-op, not local though."

Ryan washed and hulled the strawberries and scrambled some eggs, while Emily put bread in the toaster. Over breakfast they discussed some of the things they hoped to do over the summer.

Emily sat at the table, sipped her second cup of coffee. After Ryan wiped off the counter, she put her cup in the dishwasher. "Okay. So, can we go hiking now? I want to face it and get that over with."

"I'll fill our water bottles. Do you have your hiking shoes?" He figured he couldn't change her mind, so he would just go with it.

"I wore them home from the hospital."

Ryan set the water bottle on the table and sat on the couch to lace up his hiking shoes. Emily came out of the bedroom with her shoes and jacket. Ryan thought she looked pale and tired, but hoped she would take her time hiking, or give up on it if she was too tired. He grabbed his car keys and the water bottles, and they went out to his car.

Emily was quiet while Ryan drove to the Loon Lake Trail. He didn't try to start a conversation. He knew she needed some time to think this through.

There were four other cars parked in the trail lot. Ryan parked the car but did not get out. He looked at Emily. She was taking deep breaths. "You sure about this? We could do it in a couple of days."

"I'll be okay." She gave him a slight smile and climbed out of the car. Her ankle still hurt a bit, but she thought she could manage. Together, they walked to the trailhead.

"I went right last time, so let's go that way. You can lead the way."

Ryan nodded. He started off at a slow but steady pace, aware of Emily behind him. He tried to distract her, asking again about the various wildflowers they saw along the path. Usually, Emily would say, "Remember I told you that one last time" and laugh. But today she seemed to appreciate the distraction of explaining things that came easily to her.

When they got to the trail that led down to Loon Lake, Ryan stopped. "Did you go down to the lake when you came here?"

Emily nodded, and they walked down to the lake. She gestured to a log. "Last time I sat there for a few minutes and watched the loon family. I don't see them today, but let's sit here a while." She sat, and Ryan sat down beside her.

"How many little 'uns did they have this year?"

"Two that I saw. Remember last year, later in the summer, when we watched them teaching their kids to dive?"

"Yeah. The kids looked so surprised when they surfaced and didn't see their parents right away."

"They were pretty cute."

Emily stood up, ready to move on. Ryan stood, and Emily leaned against him. He put his arm around her. They stood for a moment, looking at the lake.

"Do you remember where you found me?"

"Absolutely. I don't think I'll ever forget how relieved I felt when I saw you sitting by the trail. I'll show you the tree that makes the spot when we get there."

They hiked in silence until Emily heard a rustling behind them and grabbed Ryan. "Oh, no," she whispered. He turned around and put his arms around her. And then he saw that there were two people hiking not far behind them. A man and a woman.

"It's okay, Emily. They're just hikers." He stepped off the trail and pulled Emily with him. He waited until the hikers were alongside them, then nodded, "Hey, nice day for a hike."

The hikers smiled, "Great hiking trail. Have a good one." The couple continued on down the trail.

"Sorry," Emily shivered.

"No worries. We don't have to do this today. We can head back to the car."

Emily shook her head. "Let's keep going. I'll be fine. Just a bit skittish, I guess. But I think I'm remembering something. I saw the bear, and I wasn't afraid. But soon after that, my head hurt and I heard scuffling, growling I think."

"Wow. You must have heard the bear, but it didn't seem to be attacking you. Do they eat small animals? Maybe you will remember more when we get to where we found you."

"Let's keep going."

"Do you want to walk ahead of me? I'll have your back."

"Okay." Emily started down the trail slowly, glancing back to make sure Ryan was close behind. She was beginning to tire but needed to finish this. She needed to remember.

When they reached the unused trail that branched off the main trail, they stopped and looked down the trail.

"What made you take this trail?" Ryan tried not to sound judgmental, just curious.

"It was just an impulse, I guess. I've often noticed an unused trail branching off a main trail when I was hiking and wanted to take it. Not a good idea, as it turned out."

"I know what you mean. Something unknown that might be interesting. Made sense to try it."

"I wonder if things would have turned out differently, if I hadn't taken this trail."

"Hard to say. One of those what-ifs."

They took their time walking the trail, watching out for tree roots. Emily's ankle was feeling much better, but she didn't want to injure it again.

"This is the place."

Emily turned around, and he gestured to a large oak tree next to the trail. "This is where we saw the paw prints and started searching the area on either side of the trail. It rained last night, so the prints are washed away, but I remember this tree. Recognize anything?"

Emily looked around and pointed. "Over there, a little farther down the trail. That's the pine tree that I woke up under. It seems distinctive to me, after looking at it so much. Normally, it would probably look like any other pine tree."

"You did remember the pine tree, so that's a start. Maybe more will come back to you later, after your brain processes that memory."

"I hope so. I want to look under the pine tree." She walked over to the tree and knelt down to look under it. Ryan stood on the trail and waited. "Thanks for keeping me hidden, safe." She patted the trunk of the tree and stood for a moment, listening to the chorus of birds calling to each other. She walked back to where Ryan stood. "Ok, let's go home."

They were quiet as they walked back to the car. Ryan kept a close eye on Emily and stopped to rest often. He could tell she wasn't her usual energetic self but knew she was unwilling to admit how exhausted she was.

When they got back to Ryan's apartment, Emily took a nap. She woke later in the afternoon, determined to move back to her apartment. She had felt helpless and scared out on the Loon Lake Trail, and she didn't like that feeling. She needed to take charge of things.

She could tell that Ryan was worried, as they packed up Carson's things and carried him out to the car. He wanted to change her mind, but decided he shouldn't press it.

At Emily's apartment, Ryan insisted that she take Carson in while he carried the rest of her things. When she opened the front door to the building, Reid was standing by his grandma's door. His eyes lit up.

"You brought Carson! You and Carson haven't been home."

"Do you want to hold him?"

Reid nodded and Emily put Carson into his arms. Carson rubbed his head against Reid and began to purr.

"He missed me." Reid beamed a big smile. He looked at Emily. "You know you missed those electric guys."

"Electric guys?" Emily raised her eyebrows. Some electronic game?

"Do you know those guys who are working on that apartment upstairs across the hall from you?"

"I've seen them a couple of times."

"They came around to grandma's apartment to ask us about our electricity. I guess they cut some wires or something. It didn't cut our electricity, though. That guy probably came to see you, but you weren't there."

"Maybe. Good thing your electricity was okay. I have to take Carson up to our apartment now. I hurt my ankle, and Carson and I need to rest."

"You hurt your ankle?" He looked at her and frowned. "I could help you."

"Thanks. Maybe tomorrow?"

Reid frowned. "Okay." He petted Carson once more and handed him back to Emily.

Ryan passed them on the stairs, as he took Emily's things up. He came back down and carried Carson, while Emily walked carefully up the stairs. Candace had cleared up any traces that she had stayed there.

Emily closed the drapes and noted that her plants needed watering. She would do that after she rested for a while. Emily dropped her backpack in her bedroom and lay down on the couch with Carson, while Ryan went to the grocery store to buy a few items.

When Ryan returned and put away the groceries, Carson pulled out his mouse on a wire toy and insisted they each take a turn playing with him. They laughed as he stood on his hind legs and swiped at the mouse.

Emily decided she should let her mom know that she was okay. By now her mom would have called Candace to ask about her trip, and Candace would have told her about Emily's fall. Emily didn't feel like talking about it. She didn't want to tell the whole story and would hate lying to her mom. Emily texted a picture of Carson standing on his hind legs while playing with his mouse. She wrote that she had a bump on her head, but was feeling fine, and Ryan was taking good care of her. Her mom texted back that she would like Emily to call when she felt up to it, so she could hear her voice. Emily texted that she would call tomorrow.

Later, Ryan and Emily made tacos for dinner, and Ryan cleaned up the kitchen. The two of them sat on the couch, attempting to read for a while.

Ryan put down the book he was reading. "Do you want to talk more about what happened? You could tell me more about the bear. Maybe talking about it will help you to remember more."

"I guess. It might help." Emily took a deep breath and paused for a second. "I was hiking down the trail when I saw the blue flowers that those people asked us to identify the other day. I was excited to find them, and I took a picture of them. I think I heard something. I looked along the trail to see what it was. I saw the bear standing on the trail,"

"What did the bear look like? Big? Little? Looking at you or away from you?"

"A typical black bear, medium-sized, standing sideways in the trail. It turned its head and looked right at me. I thought he or she was awesome. We just looked at each other for a few seconds. I wasn't really afraid, but I thought it might be a mama bear with cubs, and she might feel I was a threat to them. I stuck out my arms to make myself look bigger and began to sing 'The Bear Went Over the Mountain...'"

Emily stopped, frowned. "Huh. I had forgotten this part, but I felt a sudden pain, and I remember crawling off the trail. I heard some growling and thrashing about. I was scared that the bear would attack me, and I wanted to get away. It all sounds crazy."

"Not crazy. Just something that has never happened to you before. Or to most people."

"That's all I remember." Ryan noted that Emily seemed to droop, as if she had used up all of her energy.

"Enough thinking for tonight. You ready for bed?"

Emily got ready for bed and curled up on her side. Her head felt a little better, but she was still trying to find a comfortable position for sleep.

Ryan got ready for bed and lay beside her. "What did you think of the story of 'The Three Bears' when you were a kid?"

Emily laughed. "Bears keep coming up. You know, actually, I felt sorry for the bears. They were just minding their own business, and Goldilocks intruded into their space. When they came home, she caused a scene and fled."

"That's true. I kind of wished the bears and Goldilocks could be friends. Maybe Goldilocks could have apologized, and they would get along. You know how in elementary school teachers often tell you to be friends with everybody? Funny how bears have this duality. Are they cute and cuddly, or they are scary?"

"People aren't really sure how we fit into nature sometimes. We can't seem to decide whether to enjoy nature, protect it or to exploit it."

Emily put her arms around Ryan and kissed him. He kissed her back. "You okay with this?"

"Sex with you makes things better."

"Good to know."

Emily slept better than the night before but woke feeling panicked. She lay awake for a while, trying to calm down. Something lingered in her mind, like seeing something in peripheral vision that you can't quite identify, something that was dangerous.

Chapter 17

Tuesday

The young couple from Kansas opened the door to the police station and walked up to the counter. The duty cop finished talking on the phone and hung up. "May I help you?"

"Yes, my phone was stolen from my car this morning. I ran into the bakery to grab a couple of coffees and must have left it on the front seat. I didn't bother to lock the car because I thought it would just be a quick in and out. But there was some mixup at the counter with the customer ahead of me, and it took longer than I thought it would. I didn't check for the phone when I first got back into the car, but I know I put it on the seat, and we have looked all over for it." The young man looked earnestly at the duty cop.

"Okay, we'll see what we can do. Please sit there, while I find an officer to take down the details."

He walked back to the offices in the rear of the building. "There's a young couple out here to say their phone was stolen from their car."

Office Schultz looked up and frowned. "Okay, bring them back, and I'll take the particulars. Probably not much will come out of it. The phone is most likely long gone, but we'll check it out."

The duty cop nodded. He ushered the young couple back to see Officer Schultz, who introduced himself and gestured to the chairs in front of the desk. The young man launched into the story he had told at the front counter.

"I really need my phone. I've taken pictures of the trip on it. Everyone here seemed so friendly. That nice woman from the Nature Center took our picture and answered all our questions. And there was that guy who checked the air in our tire because he thought it looked low. We didn't even think about things being stolen. This isn't a big city like Kansas City."

"Well, that's true, but we do have crimes now and again. Let me take down the particulars. You should also check with your cell phone provider to see if they can give you any help in tracking the phone."

"Yeah. Already thought of that."

The couple gave their names and explained that they were recently married and on their honeymoon. The officer took their home address and an address and phone numbers where they could be reached while they were in the area.

"We'll check the area around the bakery where the phone was stolen to see if someone tossed it. If we find anything, we'll contact you. I have to warn you, though, I'm not optimistic. We'll do what we can."

"I hope you find it."

The officer ushered them back to the waiting area, sympathized with them for the theft of the phone, and repeated that he would let them know if the search turned up anything.

The young couple left the police station feeling a bit gloomier about their trip. The theft of the phone felt like a violation of their space. They decided to go out to lunch and think about what to do with the rest of the day. They checked twice to be sure that their car was locked when they got in the downtown parking lot.

Chapter 18

Emily climbed the stairs to her apartment. More tired than usual, she admitted to herself that she had gone back to work too early. She had only worked from noon until three, taking care of some paperwork and scheduling. She couldn't imagine managing students, certainly not leading a hike. She would call Brad and tell him that she needed more time off. She knew he would agree. He told her he thought she came back to work too soon.

She opened her apartment door and sensed that something was amiss. As she shrugged out of her backpack, a large figure stepped from behind the door, grabbed her, and pushed her down on the couch. Startled, she looked up to see a man wearing a black ski mask, a navy long-sleeved tee shirt, black jeans, and gloves. She screamed and shrank back against the couch.

He gestured with a gun held in his right hand. He had a gun? "Keep quiet. No one's in the building now anyway."

"Who are you? What do you want?" She placed her feet flat on the floor to stop her legs from shaking. How did he get in? How could she make him go away? He looked so sinister in that black mask.

The man sat down in a chair across from her, gun in hand. "Where's your camera?"

"My camera?" Why did he want with her camera? "I lost it."

"Where?"

Emily tried to think. What should she say? She hadn't lost it, but maybe he would believe that she had. It was at Ryan's, but she didn't want this guy to go over there. "The Loon Lake Trail, I think. I set it down to study some flowers. Later, when I looked for it, it was gone."

"I want those pictures."

"What pictures?" He must be crazy. What would he want with pictures of flowers?

How was she going to get out of here? She could scream, but Greg, who had just moved into the apartment across the hall, would have left for work about 2:30. Her neighbors in the two downstairs apartments would be at work. Reid's mom worked until 5:00. And anyone who happened to be home and came running might get shot.

What about Reid? This might be one of the days he came home with his grandmother. Emily had told him he could come over to see Carson. If his grandmother was busy, he might come upstairs without asking, even though he knew he wasn't supposed to do that. She had to get this guy out of her apartment before Reid came home.

"The ones you took at the Cliffs Trail on Monday. My boss isn't too happy that you took our picture."

"Your picture?" He was delusional. "I didn't take your picture. I took pictures of flowers and two pictures of a couple."

"You think I'll believe that? We saw you take the picture, and then you looked right at us. Who you working for? Not FBI, you're not their type. The cops or that other gang hanging around?"

"I'm not working for the cops, and I don't know anything about gangs. You must have the wrong person. Just leave quietly, and we can pretend that this never happened." She glanced around to see if there was anything with which she could defend herself.

"Nothing here to help you." He sneered at her.

The only thing she could think to do was to keep him talking until she heard someone nearby or thought of a plan. Could she throw something at him, get out the door, down the stairs, and out of the building? What about Carson? She could see him crouching on top of the refrigerator. She couldn't leave him. This man might hurt her cat.

"Ha, ha. You're funny. I'm not leaving until I get your camera and those pictures. Maybe you already uploaded them. Where's your laptop?"

"There." She pointed to the backpack on the floor by the door where she had dropped it.

He walked over, pointing the gun at her, watching. She noticed that he seemed to limp on his left leg.

As he moved to pick up the backpack, she looked at him closely. He was stocky and muscular, maybe 5' ll" and close to two hundred pounds. She couldn't see his face because of the mask, but she thought his eyes were light blue. As he waved the gun, the left sleeve of his tee shirt pulled up, and she saw a swirled tattoo that was inked down his arm.

If only she could kick the gun from his hand and turn it on him. But he was much bigger and stronger than she was, and she didn't know anything about guns or karate.

Suddenly, a white, furry body leapt from the top of the refrigerator. Carson grabbed onto the man's back, digging in his claws. The man yelled, startled, panicked. He had not seen Carson on the refrigerator, planning his next athletic stunt. The man shouted again, dropped the gun, and tried to shake Carson off.

Emily picked up the backpack and slung it into his face. She kicked the gun across the room and kicked the shin of the leg he favored. Carson jumped from the man's back and ran up to Emily. She grabbed him, opened the apartment door, pelted down the stairs, and ran out the front door of the apartment building. As she slammed the door, she heard the man cursing and stumbling down the stairs.

Carson clung to her as she raced to her car. Her keys were still in her pocket. She jumped in, set Carson down, and put the key in the ignition. She backed the car out of the driveway and turned into the street. Where should she go? A public place. That maniac still had the gun. The Food Co-op was at the end of the street, but he might shoot people there. It wouldn't be safe to go to Ryan's. The only safe place was the police station.

She stepped on the gas pedal and sped down the street. In her rearview mirror she saw her attacker standing on the porch, looking in her direction. He limped down the steps, around to the back of the house. He must have parked somewhere behind the house. She had only a few minutes lead time. She needed to get to the station as fast as she could.

At the police station, Emily pulled into the lot behind the building and parked her car with the cop cars. Her Prius looked out of place among the cruisers, but if that crazy guy was looking for her, he probably wouldn't look there. She scooped up Carson, raced to the door, pulled it open, and entered the building. Carson let out a yowl, and she released her grip. Poor cat, she was squeezing him too tightly. She was shaking so hard, she was afraid she would drop him.

"You can't bring cats in here." A patrol officer was standing by a front counter, talking to a woman sitting there.

"Why? Do you think he's hiding something underneath his fur?"

The officer scowled. "Best not to get too sassy, Miss."

"I have just been threatened by a large man with a gun, and my cat saved my life. I need to talk to Detective Perez. The cat stays with me, so maybe the detective can come down here, and you can keep an eye on the cat, so he doesn't get into trouble."

"You're serious about the man with a gun?"

"Would I make up something like that? Could you just tell Detective Perez I want to talk to her?" She took a deep breath. Her legs felt weak, and she just wanted to sit down.

The officer walked a few feet away, and she heard him explaining the situation to someone on the phone. When he finished, he walked back to where she was standing. "Come with me and tell Detective Perez what's going on."

Emily followed him down the hall and through a set of double doors. People working at their desks looked up. As she walked by, one of them smiled at the handsome white cat she clutched. At the last door, the officer gestured Emily into to an office with four desks, two of which were occupied. Detective Perez stood up from one of them. Emily did not see Detective Gibson.

"Emily, please sit down and tell me what this is about. Officer Laurentis says your cat saved your life?" Emily sat in the chair on one side of the desk, and Detective Perez sat back down on the opposite side.

"This is Carson. I need to call Ryan and have him come here. He needs to know what happened, and I'm worried about his safety." Emily brushed away the tears she felt coming at the relief of being safe.

"Okay." Detective Perez looked at her curiously and pushed the land-line phone across the desk. Emily seemed to be running on adrenaline. The detective would give her time to calm down a bit and tell her what had happened. This was not the meek young woman she had talked to at the hospital.

Emily called Ryan's number. He answered after the second ring. "Hey, how was work?"

"I am at the police station and need you to come. I'm not in trouble. I'll explain when you get here. But, Ryan, be careful. Make sure no one is watching you."

"That sounds ominous."

"Just hurry, and be careful."

"I'll be there quick as I can."

"He's coming." Without further explanation, Emily launched into her story about coming home from work and being grabbed and shoved onto the couch by a masked man who wanted her camera. Carson sat in her lap, looking at the items on the desk. Emily explained how Carson leaped onto the man's back and distracted him so she could get them both out of the apartment.

Perez whistled. "I guess Carson deserves a medal. Did you get a good look at this guy?"

"He seemed tall, maybe 6 feet, muscled. I think his eyes were blue, maybe. Oh, when his tee pulled up on his arm, I saw a swirling shape tattoo of some kind."

"Good description. And this man wanted some pictures he thinks are on your camera?"

"Seeing his guy triggered a memory for me. I think someone was there on the trail at Loon Lake that day. While I was watching the bear, I heard a rustling sound behind me. I thought it was just squirrels dashing through the woods. As I was backing up, I ran into something, or someone. Something hit me on the back of the head. I think I fell. I heard growling and shouts, so I crawled off the trail and hid behind a pine tree."

"Do you think the man who just threatened you hit you over the head on the trail and was attacked by the bear?"

"Maybe. I don't know. He said I took some pictures on the Cliff Trail. I'm sure I did, but they would have been of flowers or trees or animals, something like that."

"So, maybe you caught something else in one of your pictures, or he thinks you did. Did you take any pictures of people that day?"

"No. Oh, yes. I took a picture of a couple who were on their honeymoon." Emily thought for a minute. "I don't remember taking a picture of two men, but I did see two men as I started down the trail back to my car. I didn't give them another thought, because I was hurrying to get to work."

"So, where is the camera now?"

"It's at Ryan's."

"I'll send an officer over there to get it. If we scan the pictures you took that day, we might see what he's looking for. When we have the camera, we'll have you go through the pictures with us and see what you might have captured on film."

"Of course."

"We'll need to go to your apartment and see if we can get any fingerprints or DNA from the guy. Would you be willing to lend us your keys?"

"Sure, you can borrow the keys. He wore gloves, though, so probably no prints."

"Okay. We'll see what we can do."

Emily looked at Carson, rubbed his chin. "Carson clawed the guy. Do you think you could get enough DNA from swabbing his claws?"

Detective Perez raised her eyebrows. "There's a new idea. I've never tried that before. Do you think he would stay still for me to do that?"

"I think so. If you pet him a bit and let him know you like him, and I hold him while you swab his paws."

Perez raised her eyebrows. "He won't be able to tell that I'm not really a cat person?"

"He'll turn you into one."

"We'll give it a try. I'll get the DNA swab kit. Be right back." Detective Perez left the room.

"Okay, Carson. I know this is going to feel weird, but it won't hurt, and it might help us find that creep who barged into our apartment." She stroked Carson from the top of his head to his tail, and he rubbed his head against her.

Detective Perez came back into the room. "So, should you hold him, do you think, or set him on the desk?"

"I'll hold him, and when you're ready I'll press gently on each paw, so you can see his nails. Then just swab as gently and quickly as you can."

"Right. Hey, Carson, Emily says you are a very brave cat. And, you are the first cat I have ever swabbed for DNA." As Emily pushed gently on his front paw, Detective Perez quickly swabbed it. Carson purred as the detective swabbed each of the other paws. Then she took a damp cloth and wiped off each paw. When she was done, Carson nudged the detective's hand, and she patted his head.

"Well done, Carson. You might have made me a cat fan after all." She laughed, as Carson leaped from Emily's lap onto the desk, sat on the papers, and licked his paws. "I'll send this to the DNA lab. It should be back in a day or two, and we'll check it against our list of perps to see if we get a match. This guy sounds like he's not new to intimidation."

Emily agreed with her there. She turned as the door opened. Detective Gibson escorted Ryan into the office.

"I'm glad to see you." Emily stood up to hug Ryan, and he gave her a fierce hug back. Then he rubbed Carson's head.

"Are you two all right? What happened?" Ryan stood beside Emily, as she sat down.

"We're okay." She reached up and took his hand.

Detective Perez gestured Ryan to the second chair on the other side of her desk, next to Emily. "Emily will fill you in on what's going on. We need to discuss what to do next to keep the two of you safe."

Ryan raised his eyebrows and gave a questioning look at Emily. Keep them safe from what?

Detective Gibson leaned against the door. He wasn't sure how Detective Perez had come to be in charge here, but Emily seemed to trust her, so he would let things be for now.

Ryan squeezed Emily's hand once, when she began to recount what had happened at her apartment and her flight with Carson to the police station. No one said anything until she had finished her story. Ryan took a deep breath and shook his head. Hard to believe this could happen.

Detective Gibson looked at Emily. "Any idea who this guy might be?"

Emily shook her head. "Never seen him before, and I have no idea what he thinks is on my camera."

"First, we need to retrieve the camera. Ryan, would it be okay if a couple of officers went to your apartment to get it?"

"Sure."

"My neighbors should be warned to be careful, without scaring them too much. There are tenants in the two apartments downstairs and one upstairs in addition to mine. In one of them a mom lives with her son, a six-year-old named Reid. He sometimes waits for me in the entryway, and I don't want anything to happen to him. You should probably alert Greg, the guy who lives across from my apartment, as well."

"Good point. We'll send an officer to alert them to some robberies in the neighborhood and warn them to be careful of strangers hanging around."

"I'll see who is available to go over and get the camera." Detective Gibson left the room and came back to let them know that two patrol officers were on their way and would keep their eyes out for anyone watching the apartment.

"In the meantime, we need to keep you safe." Detective Perez turned toward Emily. "You were attacked once, and we don't yet know why. This man who seems to be worried about some pictures threatened you, and your cat. You and Ryan should move to a new location for a while, and we'll post someone to watch your apartment to see if he comes back looking for you."

"I guess that makes sense." Emily sighed. Her life had been disrupted already, and she hated the idea of moving somewhere else. But she didn't want to meet up with that man again, and she didn't want to endanger Ryan.

"We'll wait for the officers to come back with the camera, then go through the pictures from your day at the Cliffs to see if we can figure out why this guy is so worried."

"What about my car? I think he saw me drive away from the apartment. He probably already knew what car I drove, as he seems to know where I live."

"Park your car where you usually do, so he'll think you're still there. You and Ryan might want to rent a car for a week, while we look for the guy. We will find him. He can't get far."

Detective Perez stood up. "I'm going to send this DNA swab on its way. I'll leave you two to talk with Detective Gibson about where you want to go."

After Detective Perez left, Carson jumped into Ryan's lap. Ryan stroked the cat as he looked at Emily. "I came so close to losing you to some thug." He ran his hand through his hair. "It's hard to wrap my head around that."

"I was really scared. I didn't know what to do. I still feel shaky, but thanks to Carson we got out of there alive."

"Carson did his part, for sure. But you thought fast and got both of you out of the building. I can't even think about what could have happened if you hadn't."

"I'm having a hard time grasping that we were in that kind of danger. What could that guy possibly think is on my camera?"

"No idea. It sounds like we should get out of town for a while. Where could we go? We can't go to stay with friends or family, because we don't want to endanger them in this mess, whatever it is."

"I don't know. I don't want to stay in a hotel, and it's expensive." They were silent for a couple of minutes. "I have an idea. Brad has a cabin that he inherited from his family. It's on a small lake, with just a couple of other summer cabins. He lets the permanent staff at the Nature Center use it sometimes. He would probably let us use it."

"That might work. This thug we're avoiding wouldn't know about it, and we wouldn't be involving anyone else. You want to give him a call and ask?"

Emily called Brad and explained some of what was going on, not mentioning that she felt her life was in danger, just that she and Ryan would like to go someplace quiet for a few days. He assumed she needed some rest after her ordeal in the woods and having a concussion. He planned to leave work in about an hour and arranged to meet them in the parking lot downtown to give them the keys to the cabin.

Detective Gibson agreed that it sounded like a good plan and reminded them to be careful. "Hopefully, when we get your camera, we will figure out what this guy wants."

Emily nodded. She wanted this to be over. She wanted her regular life back.

When Detective Perez returned, Emily explained where they planned to stay. Emily hoped that the cops would find the guy who attacked her. She didn't want to think what they would do if he wasn't found and was still out there.

Ryan frowned. "I'm thinking about the car rental. Neither of us should drive there, as that guy or someone else might follow us. I don't want to ask someone else to take us and get them involved."

"We have a car that we sometimes use for stakeouts. Make the arrangements online, and I'll give you a ride to the car rental place."

You would do that?" Emily looked up in surprise.

"My concern is for the two of you to survive this, and for us to arrest your attacker."

"Thanks. That would solve the problem."

"I'll call the car rental and make sure we can get a car." Ryan felt in his pocket and shook his head. "I think I rushed off without grabbing my wallet. All I could think of was that you were in trouble. We could just stop by and see what cars are available, I guess."

"My debit card is in my pocket from when I went out to grab lunch for Sara and me. I'll call and reserve a car." Emily checked her phone to find the phone number of the car rental company and made arrangements for them to pick up a car in half an hour.

A patrol officer stopped by the office to drop off Emily's camera. She scrolled to the pictures she had taken on the Cliff's Trail. She had not had an opportunity to upload them, so these were the only pictures from that day. Once she found the right set of pictures, Detective Gibson transferred them to a computer, so they could get a better look.

"Wait, who are those people?" Detective Perez pointed at a young couple standing by a tree.

"I first saw them when I was standing on the lookout platform enjoying the view of the lake. After I started back down the trail, they caught up to me. They told me they were on their honeymoon and asked me to take their picture. I'm not great at taking photos of people on their phone, but they said it was fine."

"Look at the edge of the photo. Aren't there two men standing there? Can we zoom in?" She turned to Detective Gibson, who enlarged the picture.

"Let's see. There, I enlarged the image a bit, so you can see them better."

Emily gasped. "That's him, I think. The guy who attacked me!"

"You're sure?"

"Pretty sure. Same build. What do you suppose he was doing there? He didn't seem like the nature type."

Detective Perez pointed at the man whom Emily had identified and looked at Detective Gibson. "Doesn't that look like Carl, the guy we were looking for a couple of years ago in the meth bust? Something about him looks different, his hair maybe. But I think it's him."

"I think you're right. Looks like he's back in the area. I don't know that guy he's with. Beats me why they were there on the trail."

"I remember after I took the picture, Carl, if that's who he is, was looking in my direction, but I didn't think much of it. People often notice me when I'm photographing something."

"I wonder why they didn't come after you then, when they had the chance." The detective looked at Emily.

"That couple whose picture I took walked with me all the way down the trail back to our cars. They asked all kinds of questions about the area. When we got to the parking lot, I jumped in my car and left quickly. I had to get to work."

"Maybe those two men got worried that you had seen something, and Carl came looking for you. I'm not sure how he figured out who you were, but it took him a couple of days. Maybe he just got lucky and spotted you somewhere. Looks like we're dealing with a drug issue, so we'll turn that part over to the narcotics team, which will bring in the state police to look into it."

Officer Shultz walked through the room and dropped a file on a desk in the back of the room. He glanced at the computer as he passed by Detective Perez's desk.

"Hey, I talked to that couple when they came in to report that their phone had been stolen. Sorry to interrupt, but it can't be a coincidence." He turned to Emily, "Do you work at the Nature Center?"

"How did you know?"

"That couple told me how friendly everyone here is. They mentioned a nice woman who works at the Nature Center and some guy who randomly offered to check the air in their tire because it looked low."

"Wow, that's weird. I wonder what the connection is."

Detective Perez was thoughtful. "Did they describe the guy who offered to check the air in their tire?"

"Let me think. I didn't realize it was relevant, but I think they described him as a nice guy in a navy-blue hoodie."

"Wow. Carl doesn't seem like a nice guy, but could he have found out about me from them? Would that even be possible? Could he have been watching for me at the Nature Center?" Emily shook her head and shivered, freaked out that someone might have been stalking her without her knowing it. She had a vague memory of seeing such a person in the parking lot when she left work.

"Someone might be nice enough to check a stranger's tire, but that seems kind of unlikely, don't you think?" Detective Gibson looked at Detective Perez.

"Possible, but unlikely, I'd say."

"Did you find their phone that was stolen?" Ryan asked.

"Strangely, yes. It was discovered in a trash can downtown. The phone case was cracked, but it looked like it might still work. We contacted the couple, who were getting ready to go back to Kansas. They came and picked up the phone. Turned out that the young couple, who looked about thirteen to me, are a couple of tech wizards, and they thought they could make the phone work."

"Hopefully, Carl will enlighten us about the photo when we catch up with him." Detective Perez stood up and gestured to Emily and Ryan. "Okay, we'll follow you to your apartments to gather what you need to take with you to the cabin. Someone is already watching your apartment, Emily, in case Carl comes back or is watching it himself."

Emily and Ryan stood up. Ryan carried Carson, as they followed the detectives down the hall and out the back door to the unmarked car.

Chapter 19

The detectives cautioned Emily and Ryan not to touch anything more than necessary, as they would check for fingerprints and DNA. Emily packed a few things quickly, while Ryan packed up food, litter and toys for Carson and put him in his pet carrier. Carson made it clear that he did not think this was an appropriate way to honor the hero of the day, but they didn't want to risk his getting out of the car during the connections they had to make.

At Ryan's apartment, Emily and Carson stayed in the patrol car while Ryan went inside with Detective Gibson. Ryan packed a few clothes and grabbed his laptop and a couple of books he was reading for his dissertation.

Detective Perez and Detective Gibson dropped them off at the car rental, said goodbye, and told them to be safe. Ryan waited outside with their packs and an annoyed cat in a carry case, while Emily went inside.

The rental place wasn't busy on a weekday in early spring, so Emily didn't have to wait long in line. The man at the counter took her driver's license and credit card. She thought he spent more time than necessary looking at her license and back at her. Then he turned to his coworker standing at the counter next to him.

"Hey, Bill, can you take care of this? I'm not feeling well and need to leave for a minute."

Bill came over reluctantly. "What's the trouble?"

"Something I ate, I guess. I'll be back as soon as I can."

"Okay." Bill turned to Emily, quickly finished the paper-work, gave her a key and told her where to find their rental car. They found it easily and left to meet Brad.

When they drove into the parking lot, Brad was already there. He got out of his car as they pulled up.

"Thanks for the loan of your cabin. We really appreciate your help."

"My pleasure." He handed her the key. "I hope the peace and quiet out there will help you fully recover. Don't worry about coming back to work until you are really ready. There are a few essentials at the cabin, like coffee, as we like to go out there spontaneously. Use whatever you find."

"Thanks again. I'll call you when we're on our way back."

"Okay. Take care, you two." He went back to his car as Emily waved and got into the rental car.

She pulled out her phone and typed in the address that Brad had given her. Ryan drove out of the parking lot and turned left.

"This is pretty weird, but maybe it's a good thing. We can have a quiet break. Maybe I can get you to rest for a change."

From the backseat Carson made his presence known, and Emily reached back to let him out. He usually sat on her lap or walked around while they were riding in a car.

Emily talked Ryan through the directions until they were out of town and then grew quiet. When Ryan looked over, he saw that she was asleep. Carson slept on her lap, stretched out so that part of him hung off onto the seat. Ryan was sure Emily needed sleep after she had been attacked this afternoon. She had been through a lot with the concussion and the night in the woods and now the attack. Ryan felt wrung out after all the worry of the last few days, but felt he had to keep it to-gether. How had they gotten mixed up in this crazy situation?

The directions seemed clear until he got to the final stretch. Reluctantly, he woke Emily to make sure he took the correct turn.

She blinked. "Sorry, I slept."

"No problem. You needed it. I just want to check this turn. The directions seem a bit vague."

"Brad mentioned a small grocery store and gas station with a funny name." She pointed to a mint green building with a few summer chairs in the front and a large sign with balloons painted on it. "That's it, The Last Hurrah. I hope it's not our last."

"No, course it won't be. We should stop and pick up a few things, so we don't have to come back later."

"Agreed." They did not find a big selection of groceries in The Last Hurrah, but they bought supplies to last them a few days at the cabin.

Back in the car, Ryan turned right from the parking lot and continued down the dirt road until he spotted the sign for Wilson Lane.

"That's it. Turn there. Brad's mother's family were Wilsons and the cabin came from them."

The car bumped along the uneven road, and they wondered what they would find at the end of it. Trees crowded the road, and in places met overhead to create a tunnel. After a mile or so, they saw the log cabin. It looked old, but solid and well-built. It sat at the end of a small lake without a sandy beach, but with a dock and a couple of boats pulled onto the shore.

Ryan stopped the car and got out. Holding Carson closely, Emily walked up to the front door. Ryan took the key from her and wiggled it back and forth to open the door.

The living area looked more modern than the outside, with wood-paneled walls. There was a kitchen/dining area at one end of the cabin. The kitchen appliances, although not new, looked clean and well-kept. There was a large oak table with several mismatched wooden chairs. At the other end of the cabin was a fireplace with a large plaid couch and three slightly sagging but comfortable-looking chairs gathered in front of it. Firewood was stacked next to a set of fireplace tools. The cabin smelled slightly from prior fires and years of sitting in the woods. To Emily it was a comforting smell, the smell of a building that had lasted well.

Ryan went outside to bring in their belongings and the food they had bought, while Emily held on to Carson to keep him from getting outside. She and Carson checked out the two bedrooms in the back. The larger bedroom had a dresser, a queen-sized bed, a nightstand with a lamp that had a round glass base full of shells, and a bookcase with a few well-thumbed books. The other room had two sets of bunkbeds with matching quilts and two dressers. A lamp with a base in the shape of a teddy bear sat on the nightstand between the two sets of beds. Between the bedrooms there was a bathroom with a small, walk-in shower.

When Emily heard Ryan come in with the last load, she set Carson down. He immediately began his inspection tour of the cabin. After the tour, he jumped up on the plaid couch, curled up, and went to sleep.

Emily put Carson's litter box in the bathroom and then fed him. It was already dark outside, so she and Ryan opened a can of soup and ate it with some bread and cheese. Ryan opened a bottle of wine, and they took their glasses outside to check out the lake. Clouds covered most of the sky, but a half moon and a few stars peeked through. Ryan put his arms around Emily, and they stood there a few moments, enjoying the whisper of the waves against the shore.

"You must be exhausted. You're supposed to be resting, not fending off drug dealers. I should put you to bed."

Emily smiled up at him. She felt safe.

Chapter 20

Wednesday

Emily woke early the next morning, made coffee, and took it out on the porch overlooking the lake. She sat in one of the old wicker rocking chairs, which creaked as it rocked, and breathed in the moist fresh air. The fog over the water was lifting, and it looked like it would be a beautiful day. She spotted a couple of docks farther down on the lake, one with a pontoon boat tied up, but didn't see any signs there were people staying there just now.

The call of a Baltimore Oriole sounded from high up in the trees, but without her binoculars she couldn't spot it. She would love to live in a place like this and enjoy this view every morning. She didn't know if it would do for Ryan, though. He enjoyed nature, but also liked the city.

Ryan joined her on the porch holding a cup of coffee. "What do you want to do today? I feel like we're on vacation. I'm enjoying a break from not having to do anything."

"Let's see if we can walk around the lake and check out those cabins, see if anyone else is around."

"Sounds good."

Emily pointed toward the lake. "A pair of mallards. They probably have a nest around somewhere."

When they went back inside the cabin, Carson let them know he had waited long enough for his breakfast. They fed him and made scrambled eggs and toast for themselves. The kitchen area did not have a dishwasher, so they rinsed off their dishes in the large sink and set them on the counter.

Emily filled a water bottle she found in the cupboard. They took their hiking shoes outside and sat on the porch to put them on. Standing, they looked in both directions to see if they could spot a trail that circled the lake.

"I'll try the right side and you the left? There must be an old road or a trail of some kind." Ryan stepped off the porch and walked to the right.

"Okay." Emily walked to the left side of the dock. "That might be a path over here." She pointed toward a gap in the trees on the left side of the lake. "Let's give it a try."

Ryan walked over to where she stood. A narrow path ran close to the shore, where there were fewer trees. It looked as if it hadn't been used much recently. Dutchman's breeches and trailing arbutus peeked through the tall grasses that grew along the trail. Two black squirrels chased each other around and around, up and down a tree on the edge of the woods.

Farther down the trail a large log had fallen across the path. Emily looked thirty feet up a nearby trunk to a jagged break where the upper part of the tree had broken off.

"Too bad. That was a big, beautiful beech tree. I hope some of them can outlast the beech scale beetles and fungi that are eating them."

"Do they have a chance?"

"There's always a chance."

There didn't seem to be an easy way around the log, so they climbed over it. As they continued around the lake, at times they had to look closely to see where the trail contin-ued, while other times it was easy to see. At the far end of the lake, directly across from the cabin, they discovered a small, sandy beach.

"We should take out the kayak tomorrow and come over here, lie in the sand, and pretend we're at the big beach. If you feel like it, that is." Ryan looked at Emily with concern. "I'm not making sure that you rest enough."

Emily laughed. "Don't worry. If I'm about to collapse, I'll let you know."

The trail followed close to the lake for a short distance. Ryan spotted a lineup of three turtles sitting on a log that had fallen into the water. "I think those are painted turtles."

"It looks like them. But I'm just starting to identify turtles. I didn't know you knew about them."

"When I was a kid, I was obsessed with turtles. I wanted to build a pond in the backyard and stock it with turtles, but my dad wasn't into it."

Emily laughed. "Not surprising. Sounds fun, though. Why didn't you study turtles and get a PhD in them?"

"A herpetologist. I thought about it at the time. I envisioned myself scuba diving at some south seas reef and swimming with the turtles."

"That does sound exciting."

"But when I was in high school, I had this great history teacher who made history seem so relevant. He encouraged us, forced us in some cases, to keep up with current events, and then helped us to see how historic events lead to what's happening now. That really intrigued me."

"Wow. Great teacher."

"What did you want to be when you were a kid?"

"My ideas changed often. When I saw The Nutcracker, I wanted to be a famous ballet dancer. When I watched the Olympics with my mom, I wanted to be a famous ice skater. But I always wanted to study nature, and I spent a lot of time outside when I was a kid."

When they got close to the cabins on the right side of the lake, the path curved out to a two-track road. They followed the road past the cabins and picked up the trail again on the other side of them.

Farther along Ryan stopped and pointed through the trees. "Looks like some kind of old building."

Emily peered in that direction. "Oh, I see it. Let's go look and see what it is."

They climbed over a couple of small logs and swished through some ferns. Covered in vines, a small stone cabin with a partly caved in roof nestled among the trees. A few yards from the trail around the lake, it fronted onto a little-used two-track road.

Emily peered into the cabin. "It's pretty primitive, just one room, it looks like. Not much space."

Ryan looked in. "There's a fireplace at the end and maybe a wooden cot along the side."

"No windows. Looks gloomy. I wonder who lived here. It doesn't look out onto the lake. Was it just a hunting cabin kind of thing, or did someone live here year around?"

"A bit confining, I guess, but it could have been warm in the winter. Let's follow the two-track road and see where it goes. I'm guessing it goes out to the main road."

The two-track road was overgrown with grass in the middle, but the tracks were still visible. It was easier to walk in the tracks than it had been on parts of the overgrown trail. The two-track ended at a paved road. They could see one car in the distance, not much traffic.

"This looks like the main road. So, the road to our cabin must be down this road to the right." Ryan pointed in the direction he thought their cabin would be.

"Looks like it. Let's go back to the stone cabin and find the trail that leads back to our cabin."

They picked up the trail again and followed it to twenty feet from the back of their cabin. They took off their hiking shoes and left them on the porch, wanting to leave the cabin as clean as possible.

After a lunch of cheese sandwiches, carrot sticks, and packaged cookies, Emily admitted she was tired and lay down on the couch to take a nap.

Ryan sat on the porch, watching the lake, letting his thoughts wander. He remembered good times at the beach with his mom and brother and backpacking with his uncle when they had stayed in a cabin at a national park. He had always looked forward to his next birthday, but now he sometimes wished he could return to the days when the adults took care of all the hard stuff.

When Emily woke from her nap, she found him on the porch, still musing. He smiled at her, as she sat in the chair beside him.

"Just having a think out here?"

"Yeah, remembering the good old days when I was a kid and free to play and roam around with friends much of the summer, go on vacation."

"Those were good times. Life wasn't always easy, sometimes fights with friends or feeling left out, mad at my parents for some minor issue. But mostly, we were both lucky."

"Agreed."

Later in the afternoon Detective Perez called. Emily put her phone on speaker, so Ryan could listen at the same time.

"We got DNA results from the swab that we took from Carson. A match came up on our database. Carl Brander, known drug dealer. About a year ago there was a big drug bust, and a couple of meth labs were shut down. A neighbor had seen Carl going in and out of the meth house. We hoped to snare him in the bust, but he was long gone and disappeared from our radar. It appears he's back in the area, and we're looking for him. We think he's working for someone higher up the food chain, and we'd like to ensnare that person as well as Carl."

Emily paused. "Do you think he had something to do with me ending up with a concussion?"

"Here's what we think may have happened. You saw the bear, Carl hit you on the head, and you fell. Then he saw the bear and started to run, not knowing anything about how to deal with bears. You mentioned that he was favoring one leg. Maybe the bear gave chase and clawed Carl. Ryan said he and Candace found paw prints on the trail near where you were found. We checked hospitals and Emergency Care Clinics, but no one turned up with injuries that might have been caused by a bear. Carl must have gotten help from someone or treated the injuries himself. He must still be in some pain. So, just sit tight. We have alerts out. We'll find him."

"Thanks for letting us know."

"You're welcome. Everything okay there?"

"Yes, we're kind of on vacation, I guess. The cabin is fine. Let us know when you think it is safe to go home, though."

"Will do. Bye." Detective Perez cut off the call.

"I don't believe this is happening." Emily looked at Ryan.

"Me either. Drug dealers? We don't live in the big city. It's supposed to be peaceful up here." He put his arms around Emily, and she hugged him tightly.

"Do you think we're safe here?" Emily looked up into Ryan's face.

"Yeah, I think so. They didn't follow us, and it's so remote out here. No one else around. I don't see how they could possibly know that we left town in a rental car."

"Seems not. I still feel a bit anxious, though. I'm trying not to be."

"Like Detective Perez said, we'll sit tight here until they find that guy they called Carl."

Ryan made sure the cabin's windows and doors were locked before they went to bed. Just to be on the safe side.

Emily awoke in the night, thinking she heard something, or someone, outside. She listened, but heard only the lapping of waves against the shore and the wind in the pine trees. Just her imagination. Carson had nudged his way between her and Ryan and stretched out lengthwise. She stroked the length of his body and went back to sleep, as he began to purr.

Chapter 21

Thursday

The next morning, Ryan and Emily slept in, and then took their breakfast out to the porch. Although clouds gathered on the horizon, sun shone through the trees and sparkled like gems on the lake.

"More coffee?" Emily took the cup Ryan handed her and returned with refills. "Do you want to take out the kayak?"

"Sure. I'd like to see the rest of the lake."

Later, they went down to the lake and turned over the two-person kayak. It looked well-designed and gently used. They pushed it out into the water, Emily sitting in the front seat and Ryan sitting in the back.

The lake was calm, and they soon reached a companionable rhythm as they dipped paddles in and out of the water. Paddling along the edge of the lakeshore, they checked out the other docks. No one else seemed to be staying at the lake this early in the season.

Just ahead of them two small heads popped out of the water. "Hey! Those look like otters. I've always wanted to see some in the wild."

"Wow. How cool." Ryan looked in the direction she pointed, where two heads bobbed in the water.

As they paddled forward, the heads disappeared and then reappeared farther down the lake. When the kayak got closer, the otters darted down into the water and their heads reappeared farther along. Ryan and Emily laughed, as they slowly followed the otters to the end of the lake. Then the otters disappeared underwater, and Emily and Ryan did not see them surface again.

"That was a fun game. They weren't afraid of us at all. I've always heard that otters are playful."

"Wonder if we'll see them on our way back to the cabin."

"Hope so."

At the other end of the lake, they pulled the kayak up on shore and sat on the small sandy beach. Ryan leaned back and closed his eyes, enjoying the warmth of the sun. Emily closed her eyes and listened to identify bird calls.

When a cloud covered the sun, she opened her eyes and gazed out over the lake. Suddenly, she grabbed Ryan's arm. "There's someone at our cabin."

"What?" Ryan peered around the kayak. "Who could it be? Maybe a neighbor come to check us out?"

"Oh, my gosh, do you think those drug guys could have found us somehow?" Emily shivered.

"Here, take the binoculars. See if you recognize the guy who attacked you."

Emily trained the binoculars on the man standing on the porch of the cabin. "I think it's him. Ryan, we have to do something. Carson is inside!" As she watched, another man came up unto the porch. "There are two of them." She found she was whispering, as if the drug dealers could hear her.

"He'll be okay. Carson is really smart. He'll find a place to hide, and they won't find him." Ryan really hoped that was true. He didn't want to think what would happen if the dealers found their cat. "We have to try to find that trail we were on yesterday and get back there. Maybe they won't be sure we're staying there and will leave."

"I hope you're right." Emily's eyes filled with tears. Their only chance to save Carson was to get back to the cabin without those guys seeing them. "We have our phones. Our laptops and my purse are in the trunk of the car. I can't think of anything else that they could use to identify us. Can you?"

"I left my wallet in the glove compartment. So, no, I don't think they could tell who was here." Ryan peered across the lake, keeping behind the kayak. "I don't think they can see us from this far away, if we stay close to the ground. Come on. We'll crawl back into the trees. Keep the kayak between the trees and the other end of the lake."

Heart pounding and going easy on her sprained ankle, Emily crawled after him into the nearby trees. They crouched behind some bushes and watched.

"We should sneak along the lake, past the empty cabins, until we get near our cabin. You hide, while I make noise and then start running through the woods. They'll think we're both running away and will follow me."

"Are you crazy? Do you think I'm going to let you get yourself killed, while I get away?"

"I'm not going to get killed." To himself, Ryan hoped that would be true. "You had a concussion, remember? You aren't in any condition to outrun anybody. I'm sure I can run faster than they can. Remember that guy who attacked you has an injured leg."

"What about the other guy? I didn't see him very well, but he looked taller and wasn't limping."

"I'll be fine. I used to run track, remember?" He hadn't actually told her that he was not the most successful runner on the team. But he was a fast runner, even faster when he was terrified.

"Remember yesterday, when we walked the trail around the lake and found that old stone building on a two-track road? And we discovered that road goes out to the main road? I'll dash down the trail to get their attention. When I get to the stone cabin, before they are able to see me, I'll dash over to the two-track and run out to the main road. They will be running in the opposite direction around the lake and back to the cabin. I'm hoping they won't see the two-track until they get to the two cabins where the trail stops. That will give me a little extra time. You go into the cabin and grab Carson. Then get to the car and take off. I'll meet you at the main road."

"I don't know, Ryan. What if they have guns?"

"They won't be able to get a good shot at me, and they won't know I'm on the two-track headed out to the main road. Anyway, it's our only chance to get out of here. Do you think you can find the two-track after you get the car?"

"We figured it was the first road past the drive to the cabin. I'll try to find it, but what if I don't?"

"You will. I'll meet you there."

"Oh, Ryan, I don't like it."

"Neither do I, but we have to try it. First, we have to get to the cabin, so let's find our way there."

As quietly as they could, Emily and Ryan crept down the trail toward the cabin, stepping into the trees to avoid being seen. The two men had gone inside, so they should have a brief period of time during which the men would not be looking in their direction. Maybe enough time to get back to the cabin without being discovered.

When they were near the cabin, Emily found a bush to hide behind where she couldn't be seen from the cabin or from the trail, when the men ran down it. Ryan sneaked past the cabin, stepped on a branch and rustled through some downed leaves until he heard a shout.

"There they go. Let's get 'em."

Ryan dashed down the trail, running faster than he thought he had ever run. If he had had drug dealers on his trail, he might have won some medals at the track meets. He tried to pace his breathing and ease his feeling of panic.

Emily held her breath and made a wish for Ryan, as the two men ran past the cabin after him. She noted that her attacker was slow, but the other guy looked younger and was a better runner. When they were out of sight, she raced to the cabin and entered through the back door.

"Carson, where are you?" She scanned the kitchen and living area but didn't see him, then checked the two bedrooms. He wasn't there. Her heart pounded, and she could barely breathe, fearing that she would find Carson's body. What would she do if she did? She couldn't think about that. She had to stay calm, get Carson, and save Ryan.

She ran into the bathroom, turned in a circle, and heard a meow. Looking up, she saw an opening in the ceiling where a furry white head peered down at her. She stood on the edge of the bathtub and reached up. Carson jumped into her arms.

"Come on, Carson, we have to find Ryan." She grabbed her jacket with the keys in it and raced to the car, holding Carson. She jumped in, set Carson on the passenger seat, and started the car.

The drug dealers' car, a Ford SUV, was parked in the driveway right behind their rental car. She would have to maneuver around it, driving on the grass to get onto the driveway. She backed up and started around the right side of the SUV. The tree on that side was too close. She'd never get the car through that space. She backed up again and started around the other side, clenching her jaws in frustration. She had to get to Ryan. It was a tight fit for the car. Why did people drive these big vehicles, anyway? At least the Ford was silver, like the rental car, so maybe the paint wouldn't show on the rental if she scraped it. Stupid thought!

She eased through the narrow space past the Ford, and pulled onto the gravel road. She pushed the car as fast as the rough road would allow, out to the main road. She turned left and sped down to where she thought the old two-track road would meet the highway.

Ryan continued to run, cutting into the trees off the trail, jumping over downed logs, hoping he could make it to the main road. The trail curved back and forth, so he didn't think the dealers could see him.

"There he is!"

Hearing the shout, he ran faster, watching for the stone cabin through the trees. When he glimpsed it, he raced over to it and hid behind it until he heard them run past him down the trail in the opposite direction he intended to go.

The clouds now covered the sun, and it seemed darker than usual for afternoon. He heard thunder in the distance, and the wind suddenly picked up. He thought he felt a couple drops of water on his head. Great, a downpour would slow him down. But it would slow down the drug dealers too.

He ran down the two-track toward the main road. He wanted to stop and take a deep breath, but he knew there was no time. If his dad were here, he would be shouting directions about Ryan's running style. But Ryan wasn't running for style. He was running for his life. If he didn't make it, he hoped Emily would take off and get to safety.

Emily shot past a two-track road, thought maybe that was the right one, and backed up. She pulled to the side of the road and left the car running, drumming her fingers on the steering wheel, breathing heavily. What if she wasn't in the right spot? What if Ryan didn't come? She told herself to breathe slowly, it would work out, because she didn't know what she would do if it didn't.

Emily sensed the light darken, as the clouds won out over the sun. A couple of raindrops fell on the windshield. She continued to tap her fingers on the steering wheel, impatient to see Ryan and know he was okay.

A distance behind him, Ryan heard another shout. The drug dealers had realized he wasn't in sight. They must have found the two-track and seen him farther down it. He hoped he wouldn't hear a gunshot. Being shot would hurt a lot. And slow him down, he joked to himself. No time to think about it. Just keep running.

Ryan saw the main road ahead through the trees. He dashed out from the two-track and looked around for Emily. He saw the car, ran to it, and jumped in.

The rain suddenly pelted down, obscuring the view out the windshield. Emily turned up the wiper speed.

"Go, go. They spied me on the two-track and are not far behind me."

Emily floored the gas pedal and sprayed gravel, as the car sped down the road. In the rearview mirror she saw the taller drug dealer dash out of the two-track and wave a hand in their direction. A gun? But they were now too far away. She continued watching in the mirror to see Carl emerge, but he didn't appear.

Suddenly Ryan grabbed the wheel and gently pulled the car to the right. "The car was drifting across the center line. You okay?"

"I was watching for Carl, but he didn't appear back there."

"He probably couldn't make it with his injured leg."

Tears of relief streamed down her face. They had made it! She reached over and grabbed Ryan's hand. "I was never so glad to see anyone in my life."

"Well, that's a good sign." Ryan squeezed her hand. "I wasn't sure if I would make it. But we're safe. They will have to go back to get their car, and we'll be long gone."

Emily wiped the tears with her hand and gave a shaky laugh. "This is the craziest thing that has ever happened to me. We need to call Detective Perez. I want them to catch these guys."

"I'll call her after I catch my breath." Ryan leaned back in the seat. His heart was beating wildly, and now that he was safe, he could hardly breathe. After a few minutes of silence, his breathing slowed enough to talk.

"Those guys know what kind of car we're driving and will assume we're headed home, so we should go another direction." Ryan looked at the map from the glove compartment. "There's a side road about a mile ahead that would take us to the other end of town from where they would expect us to drive. I'll watch for it." He called Detective Perez.

"Hello, Ryan? Everything okay?"

"Detective Perez. We're on our way back. The drug guys found us at the cabin, and we made a quick escape."

"How could that be? We've been so careful. Are you okay? Where are you now? Where are the drug dealers?"

"We outran them, and they aren't on our tail at the moment. I don't think they'll be able to find us."

"Thank goodness for that. Did you get the make and license number of their car?"

"Hey, Emily, did you get the make or license number of the drug dealer's car?"

"Let me think. I was so focused on meeting you." She remembered trying to drive around the Ford. What had it looked like? "It was a silver Ford, certainly bigger than a Prius. A sporty SUV, I think. The license number started with three letters that could be a word. Maybe LIT?"

Ryan relayed the information, and Detective Perez told them to come to the police station. She would send out alerts to all officers to look for the drug dealers' car.

Emily concentrated on driving, while Ryan gave her directions. She continued to look in the rearview mirror for the silver SUV. Nothing.

The next time she looked, she saw a big, silver vehicle bearing down on them. She yelped, "It's them!"

"What?" Ryan turned and looked out the back window. "Just another silver vehicle. Probably some jerk in a hurry."

"No, I'm sure. It's them. Carl must have gone back for the car!" Emily was shaking. "Oh, my gosh."

"We'll be okay." How would they be okay against drug dealers with guns? "Drive faster. Try to get to the road we're looking for. If they catch up before then, slow down as fast as you can and let them pass us." Ryan wasn't sure how to manage a chase. It looked easy on TV. Maybe they could figure out something. They had to.

Emily pushed down on the gas until she was traveling at a speed faster than she had ever driven before. She wasn't usually a fast driver and was terrified that she would crash the car. The tires planed on the rain-slick road.

The SUV was gaining, but Emily didn't think she could go faster. It was almost on their bumper and started to pass. Emily hit the brake, throwing her and Ryan forward in the seat, but not triggering the airbags. She saw Carl brandish a gun in their direction, but just then they got to the side road they were looking for. Emily turned the steering wheel to the right, and they careened around the corner. The car fishtailed. Just past the turn, a two-track road led to the left.

"Turn there!" Ryan yelled.

Emily threw the wheel to the left, and the car slued through the sandy two-track road until they were behind some trees. Ryan turned around and watched the road behind them until he saw the SUV fly past the two-track road they had just turned down.

"Turn around, drive back down to the main road, and turn right. We'll head in the opposite direction they just went. Hopefully, it will take them a couple of minutes to realize we're not on that road."

Emily backed the car up. Hands shaking, she nudged the car forward until she was able to turn it around. Back at the side road, she turned right and drove back to the main road.

"I think I see them way back there, coming this way."

She stepped harder on the gas, ran the stop sign, and turned left. Within seconds she saw whirling blue lights in the rearview mirror. "It's a cop! He's after us!?"

Ryan turned around and looked back. "Unbelievable! They should be after the drug dealers instead of us."

Emily slowed down and pulled the car onto the side of the road. She slumped in the seat, drained of energy. The rain stopped suddenly.

"What should we tell the cop? We're outrunning drug dealers? Who would believe such an explanation?"

"Let's just play along. We'll get a ticket, but Detective Perez can help us out. In any case, a ticket is the least of our worries right now."

Emily nodded.

The police car parked behind them. After a few seconds, an officer got out of the car and walked slowly up to the driver's window. Emily rolled down the window.

"Do you realize you ran a stop sign back there?"

"Yes, sorry."

"Do you drive down this road often? Do you know the speed limit on this road?"

"No, not really. I've never been on this road before."

"Is this your car?"

"No, it's a rental car."

"Driver's license and registration, please."

Ryan pulled the packet with the registration information from the glove compartment and passed it to the officer.

"My license is in my purse, in the trunk."

The officer nodded. "Open the trunk and then step out of the car, slowly."

Emily fumbled to find the lever that opened the trunk. The officer gestured for her to get out of the car. She got out slowly, walked back to the trunk, and took her license from her purse. She handed it to the officer.

Just then a silver Ford sped by them. "It's them." Emily pointed and yelled.

The officer looked at her. "How much have you had to drink, ma'am?"

Emily was startled. "Nothing."

"Get back in the car, ma'am. I'll be right back." The officer walked to the patrol car, as his radio began to beep.

Emily got back into the car and looked at Ryan. "Did you see them go by?"

"I saw them. At least they won't be chasing us with a cop car parked behind us."

"The officer asked me how much I had to drink." Emily stopped and put her hand over her mouth to stop from laughing hysterically.

"I wish we had been drinking instead of running from drug dealers."

The officer came back to the driver's window. "Here's your license and registration. Drive carefully on your way home." He hurried to his car and peeled out with his siren blaring.

"I think he got the message."

They sat quietly in the car. Ryan took a deep breath. "You want me to drive for a while? We shouldn't have to worry about the drug dealers. I'd think they would want to get as far away as they can. I'm not sure where we are. Let's just put in our address and follow directions home."

Ryan pulled the car onto the road and followed the directions toward home. They were silent for a few miles.

"I think we should find an apartment together, one with more space than what we have now." Emily glanced at Ryan.

"That was sudden." Ryan smiled. "Great idea, though."

Emily smiled back. "I can't think of anyone I'd rather escape from drug dealers with."

"Well, that's certainly a compliment."

"I was worried that when you finish your dissertation and get your degree, you won't want to stick around here. And then it will be be so complicated to figure out."

"Whatever happens, we'll find a way to make it work."

"No way to know what might happen, so let's enjoy it while we can."

Chapter 22

At the police station Emily carried Carson inside. This time no one questioned his presence.

A police woman walking by reached out to rub Carson's head. "Hey, Hero Cat. How are you?"

In spite of the seriousness of what was happening, Emily smiled. "Is Detective Perez here?"

"Yeah, come on. Glad you made it back. I'll take you to the detective."

Emily was surprised that the police woman knew who they were, even about Carson. Their story must have made it around the station. Probably not surprising, since things like this didn't happen much here.

Detective Perez stood up when they entered her office. "I'm relieved to see you. I had no idea those dealers would be able to find you. But good news. There were a couple of local cops out in the area of the cabin where you were staying. They heard our APB and spotted the car with the drug dealers. When they reported the location, the state police were able to intercept them, and the dealers are both in custody."

Emily and Ryan looked at each other. Emily collapsed in a chair. "That's good news. I can't believe it's over." She trembled, and took a deep breath. Ryan stood beside her and squeezed her shoulder. His adrenaline rush had faded, and he was exhausted.

Detective Gibson walked into the room and leaned against the desk next to Detective Perez. "You made it."

"So, I think you're safe," Detective Perez continued. "We'll need you to make a formal identification, but that can wait. You probably want to go home now."

Emily nodded. "Enough excitement. How did those guys know we were at the cabin? I thought we outsmarted them."

"As yet, we don't know. We've asked Detective Jeffers, our tech guy, to look into it. It seems there are lots of ways for people to track each other these days."

"Carl and his pal may provide some information when we question them. And there are a couple of persons of interest who we're talking to. That's all we can say for now. We'll let you know when we have things figured out." Detective Gibson nodded at them.

"Just glad we're done with it."

Detective Perez came around the desk and shook their hands. She rubbed Carson's head as well. "Thanks to all three of you for your help and your quick thinking. I'm sorry you had to go through all this, but hopefully, we got some drug dealers off the street."

"Thanks for believing what we said and finding out what was going on."

"Detective Gibson and I will follow you home and check everything out to be sure there's no one else around. Just a precaution. Send me the directions to the cabin where you were staying. We'll take a look around, check for fingerprints, pack up whatever you left there, and bring it back."

"I almost forgot we had left our stuff there. I guess nothing we can't live without."

"We'll be going out there today, so it won't be long before you get your things back. We need to contact the owner to let him know we'll be there."

Emily and Ryan suddenly looked at each other. "Brad," they said at the same time.

"We used his cabin, and drug dealers showed up. He knows nothing about that." Emily shifted in her seat. "Let us talk to him before you tell him."

The detective nodded. "As long as you do it soon."

Emily handed Carson to Ryan and pulled her phone out of her jacket pocket. She stood up and left the room. Ryan followed her. Brad answered the phone. Trying to sound calm, Emily told him they had returned from the cabin and asked if she and Ryan could come and talk with him.

Emily hoped nothing had gone wrong at the cabin while the drug dealers were inside. The cabin was old. Brad said it had been in the family for generations. It meant a lot to him. His oldest son was off to college in the fall, and his daughter wouldn't be far behind. Brad and his wife were determined to help their kids pay for their education, so they wouldn't be lost in debt when they graduated. Extra money to fix damage to the cabin would not be easy to find.

Emily and Ryan went back into the office and told the detectives that they were going to the Nature Center to explain everything to Brad.

"We can give you about thirty minutes, and then we'll be right behind you. We need to get to the cabin and check for evidence ASAP." Detective Gibson looked eager to get at it.

The detectives followed Ryan and Emily out to the parking lot. They drove to Ryan's apartment to be sure no one suspicious was lurking about, then checked out Emily's apartment. They would have a patrol officer check regularly for a few days to be sure that no one else involved with the drug dealers was around.

When Emily and Ryan arrived at the Nature Center, Sara was putting things away before going home. Surprised to see them, she gave Emily a hug and welcomed them back from their stay at Brad's cabin.

"I thought you'd probably stay longer. You know, great chance to relax and be alone."

Emily shook her head. "Well, something came up. We need to talk with Brad. We told him we were coming."

Sara frowned. "Is there something wrong. Are you okay?"

Emily gave a short laugh. She wasn't sure she would ever be okay again. "I'd like you to come with us to talk with Brad. You need to hear the whole story. Where's Mike? He should hear this, too."

"I'll call him. He's out on the trail somewhere." She picked up her phone.

In Brad's office Emily and Ryan sat down across the desk from him, and Sara pulled in a chair from another office. A few minutes later, Mike eased in through the door and leaned against the wall.

Emily launched into the whole story, starting with when she met the young couple from Kansas and took their picture. Ryan added a few details. Sara's eyes got wider, as they explained what had happened. Brad sat forward in his chair.

"I am so sorry, Brad. We should have told you why we were going, but we didn't want you to be involved. The detectives thought we should keep everything quiet, so no one else would be in danger."

"If they did any damage to the cabin, of course we'll pay for it." Ryan leaned back in his chair, glad that everything had been explained. "The detectives will be here any minute to tell you they're going out to the cabin to check for evidence. We're so sorry to put you through this."

"Not to worry. I'm sure all will turn out okay. You two should go home and get some rest. You can pick up your things from the cabin whenever you feel up to it."

Emily grimaced. She didn't really want to go back there. The cabin that had seemed so peaceful now seemed menacing. "Detective Perez said they would bring back our stuff."

Sara looked at each of them. "Hey. Let's have a cabin clean up party. Brad's family, Mike and Zac, Jeremy and me with our daughter. We can all clean things up and then have a cookout. The kids can take out the kayak, hike around the lake. That will change how everyone feels about the place."

"That's kind of you." Emily looked at Brad to see what he thought. Maybe he didn't want a lot of people there.

Brad nodded. "Okay, Kate and I have talked about inviting all the Nature Center staff to the cabin. Our summer interns haven't started yet, but we can have another get-together later in the summer. I'll ask her what she thinks."

"How about this Saturday, if it's okay with Kate. I'll see if Mike and Zac are available and organize everything. Kate will help, I know. She's a great party planner."

Back at her apartment Emily took a shower, while Ryan went to the store to get litter and cat food, as they had left all that at the cabin. This was the first time she had been in her apartment for any length of time since Carl had been there. It felt weird, almost like the scene had never happened.

Later, they sat on the couch and shared a bottle of wine. Ryan put his arm around Emily, and she leaned against him. Carson stretched out between them, his head on Emily's lap.

"I wonder if this was a Reid day. He'll be worried about Carson, since he hasn't seen him for a couple of days. Tomorrow I'll talk to his grandma and find a time for him to visit. If I move out of my apartment, what will I tell Reid? He'll be heartbroken if he can't see Carson."

"We'll have to think about that. He could come and visit Carson at our new place. It'll take a while to find a place that we want. We'll figure it out."

"I wish his mom could get him a cat. But I understand why she doesn't want one more thing to take care of. Maybe I can convince his grandma to get a cat for Reid at her place."

When the detectives arrived at the Nature Center to talk with Brad, Sara showed them back to his office. Brad stood up and shook hands with them. He gestured to the chairs in front of his desk.

"Emily and Ryan said you need to go to my cabin to look for evidence. I'd like to go with you. I want to reassure myself that my cabin is still intact and assess the damage, if any."

"Okay. Do you want to drive separately or go with us?" Detective Gibson didn't blame the guy for wanting to check on his cabin.

"I'll take my own car, and you can follow me. I'll write down the directions, though, in case we get separated. You might not find the address easily, if you put it into your phone app."

"We should get started. I'll need directions from you to give to our forensic guys, who will meet us there to check for fingerprints and other evidence."

Brad wrote out the directions, and Detective Gibson sent them to the team that was meeting them. Brad drove his car and the detectives followed him. Brad listened to his favorite radio station to ease his anxiety that something terrible had happened to his grandfather's cabin. He knew it was an old cabin, but it had a lot of happy memories of family times spent there. When he had inherited it, he had updated it but left much of it the same as it had always been.

They passed The Last Hurrah, turned down the road to the cabin, and parked their cars. Brad got out and looked at the cabin. The outside looked okay. He waited for the detectives to go inside. They had told him that he should not touch anything before it had been checked for evidence.

The forensics team arrived just after they did. They didn't plan an extensive search, since Carl and his co-dealer had not been at the cabin long. They dusted for prints, photographed footprints, and picked up a couple of cigarette butts they found in the yard.

When the forensic team left, the detectives took Brad inside. He looked around and was relieved to see that the drug dealers had made a quick foray in and out. Fortunately, they had not stayed after Ryan and Emily had driven away.

Chapter 23

Friday

In the morning Emily and Ryan returned the rental car and then went to their own apartments. They had decided to spend some time alone, to put their lives back together and think through what had happened.

Emily hoped to return to work on Monday. She spent the day cleaning her apartment, doing laundry, and trying to get back to normal. After he checked the apartment to make sure all was in order, Carson took a nap in a spot of sun.

As she was taking laundry out of the dryer, Emily mused about her time alone in the woods and the memories that had come back to her when she had been unable to walk out. She got up from the couch and went into the bedroom. She opened the closet door and looked at the violin case that was pushed back into the corner. Why had she given up playing it? Thinking about Andy reminded her how much she had loved the violin. In high school she had taken lessons, and in her senior year she had played first chair violin in the orchestra. In college she had moved on to focus on new relationships and what career she should pursue.

She pulled out the case and dusted it off. When she took out the violin, she found that its strings were still intact, but it was definitely out of tune. She sat on the bed and gently tuned the strings, checking them with her tuner. It took some time to tighten them enough so the violin sounded as it should. She pulled the bow across the strings and began to play a simple tune that she still remembered.

In the afternoon Detective Perez called. "I'm hoping you and Ryan can come into the station. We have some information that I think will be of interest to you."

Emily said that she would call Ryan and they would come to the station in an hour.

"Hey, how's it going?" Ryan sounded relaxed. How are you doing?"

"Okay, a bit shaken, but relieved to be home. Detective Perez called. They want us to come down to the station to give us some information. In about an hour?"

"Sounds interesting. I'll pick you up."

Detective Gibson met them at the front desk and ushered them back to the detectives' office. He gestured them to sit down. Detective Perez greeted them and let Detective Gibson take the lead.

"We've talked with our two drug suspects. Carl has lawyered up and isn't talking. But the new guy is cooperating for a reduced sentence. I think he has decided the drug life is not what it's cracked up to be. It turns out that Carl was out of town for a few days, and Dan followed you to keep track of you while Carl was gone."

Emily gasped. "The guy at the beach who was watching Candace and me."

Ryan frowned. "What guy?"

"Candace saw him. She thought he was watching us, but I didn't think anything of it."

"Probably him, then." Detective Gibson continued. "It also turns out that Dan works for the car rental company. A bit of luck for him and Carl. The rental company called us this morning to report that they found a tracking device on your rental car after you returned it." He sat back and let that bit of information sink in.

"You're kidding. He was there when I rented the car?" Emily sat forward in her chair. "Oh. The guy who waited on me kept looking at me and at my license. He said he felt sick and asked the other guy there to take care of me."

"That would explain how he knew which car you were renting and could put on the tracking device."

"Why didn't they follow us right away to the cabin?" Emily frowned.

"Because Dan had to wait until Carl came back into town for them to go looking for you. We think it wasn't just about the pictures on the camera. We think Carl wanted to shut you up. He seemed to think you knew something."

"I really didn't know anything at all. I didn't pay any attention to Carl on the trail that day, and I don't know anything about the drug trade." Emily sighed.

"Carl was a bit paranoid after the meth bust, when someone identified him to us. He wasn't taking any chances, I guess. As an aside, Ryan, his cohort Dan was a track star in high school, known for his speed as a runner."

"Just my luck. What happened to him? How did he get mixed up with drug dealers?"

"We understand he sustained an injury in a car accident. He took drugs for the pain, and one thing led to another."

"How sad." Emily frowned.

"True. It happens. Too often. We should check both of your cars to see if Carl or Dan planted tracking devices on them. That would explain how they knew where you lived."

Ryan and Emily stared at her. Ryan shook his head. "Why didn't we think of that? To me, tracking devices are part of the plots on TV shows, they don't happen in real life."

"Those things happen more than you might think."

Chapter 24

Saturday

Emily woke up early. She had slept well, feeling safe and at home. She left Ryan asleep, while she took a shower and made coffee. He came out into the kitchen. "Ready for the big cleaning day at the cabin?"

Emily shook her head. "Not really. You?"

"No, but it's a good idea. I'll feel better about everything, I think. And it's only fair to Brad. Sara saved us by suggesting we all come out to help."

For the picnic she and Ryan had tossed a large salad and baked sugar cookies in the shapes of animals for the kids who would be there.

When they arrived at the cabin, Brad was already there with his wife Kate and his two teenagers, Kevin, who was 15 and Marcie, who was 17. He had bribed them with the chance to kayak. Their family had spent a lot of time at the cabin and his kids had always loved it.

Sara was there with her husband Rich and their daughter Sasha, age three. Sara and Kate organized everybody, while Rich played with Sasha and Brad started the charcoal. Brad's kids were already pushing the kayak out into the lake, splashing each other with their paddles. Brad had told them they didn't have to help with the cleaning. He was just glad they were willing to come. There might not be many more times in the near future when they were willing to come with their parents.

Mike and his partner Zac arrived just as Sara divided up the cleaning tasks. The cabin wasn't in bad condition, so they figured together they could clean it quickly and then eat.

Since Zac worked at one of the local wineries, he and Mike had brought a few bottles of their favorite wines, as well as a couple of six-packs of beer.

The cleanup didn't take long. Mike had brought music on his phone, which he hooked up to speakers. They took turns choosing songs while they worked. Brad and Rich had pulled all the outdoor furniture from the shed and hosed it off.

Kevin and Marcie found some of their old sand and water toys in the shed, laughing at memories of times they had played at the cabin with their cousins when they were younger. Sasha was awed by the two teenagers, who played with her while her parents took out the kayak.

Emily and Ryan slipped away to hike around the lake and chase away the bad memories of the last few days. They walked the trail that Ryan had run to distract the drug dealers. They looked again at the stone cabin they found on their first walk around the lake.

"How are you feeling? Does this bring it all back?" Emily put her arm around Ryan.

"I was terrified when I was running, afraid what might happen, worried about you. But part of me felt like I was watching it all happen to someone else."

"I know the feeling. You were very brave to outrun them. You saved us."

"You did your part. And we made it." They stopped and just held each other for a few minutes. Then they walked back to the cabin.

Mid-afternoon, everything was packed up and put away. They said goodbye and got into their cars. Emily and Ryan again thanked Brad for the use of the cabin. He assured them that all had turned out well. They both hugged Sara, grateful that she organized a party to help chase away bad memories.

When they got back to Emily's apartment, they fed Carson. Emily organized her flower photos and Ryan read. Emily thought about all that happened.

"I think I remember more clearly what happened out on the trail. About the bear, I mean."

"Like what?"

"I remember seeing the bear. He or she looked right at me. At first I was just stunned and I didn't feel scared. I held out my arms to look bigger and started to sing. The next thing I remember, I woke up in that depression off the trail. I didn't know how I got there. The weird thing is I had been dreaming that you were lying beside me. And I realized that my back really was warmer than the front of me."

"Dreams can feel pretty real sometimes."

"That's true. Another thing, though. Do you think the bear attacked Carl to protect me? That sounds really nutty, doesn't it? Must be the concussion talking."

"Well, it doesn't seem likely, but if you want to think so, it doesn't do any harm. It's a nice thought."

"Thanks. I was worried that maybe my brain was permanently damaged."

Ryan smiled. "I think your brain is strained, but recovering. You've managed to keep going and work things out through all this crazy stuff. You'll be fine."

Emily squeezed his hand. "Thanks. Hope you're right."

"You know, the DNR has been out on that trail, looking for the bear. The DNR officers thought maybe they should move him or her farther away from people. If it was a she-bear with cubs, that would be more complicated. But no one has seen any sign of it."

"I wish the bear well, in any case. It probably saved my life, whether if intended to or not."

"Here's to the bear, then." Ryan raised his glass, and Emily clinked hers to it. Carson stood up, stretched, and rubbed his head against Ryan's hand. "Okay, Carson, you're right. You saved Emily too, so here's to cats as well."

"What about you? Want to talk more about how you felt when you were running from the drug dealers?"

Ryan took a deep breath. "I hate to admit how scared I was. But part of me was in the zone, just running as fast as I could. Even when I thought about getting shot, the situation didn't really feel like reality."

"Getting shot. That's a frightening thought." She leaned against him.

"Knowing you and Carson were waiting for me helped. That kept me focused. As if I would disappoint you if I didn't make it."

"That would have terrified me, more like. I sat there in the car, worrying I was parked at the wrong road, worrying something would happen to you and I wouldn't know about it." She shivered.

"We both made it. That's what I try to remember."

"Me, too."

Emily and Ryan sat in companionable silence, Ryan stroking Carson's head and Emily listening to his comforting purr. Ryan shifted his position to look at Emily.

"Are you going to tell Candace and your mom what happened? Candace will want to know, for sure."

"I'll tell Candace but I don't know how much I'll tell Mom. She'll just worry about me. What about you? Will you tell your family?"

"Maybe. Not just yet, though. I need to let it settle in a bit for me first."

"Do you think we will ever be the same after all this crazy stuff that interrupted our lives?"

"Probably not just the same. But life will settle back down to normal eventually, although normal may look different."

"I keep asking myself, should I be more careful now? You know, not hike alone, always carry a phone, don't talk to strangers, look over my shoulder more often."

"I can see that. Or, we could just live for today, enjoy life, take risks, do what we want to do, because life is short, and we never know what might happen. You know, should we climb mountains in Nepal, should we travel the world?"

"That's another option. It's appealing in lots of ways. I don't think I could afford it, though. It's harder, I think, to be thoughtful and disciplined, rather than impulsive."

"We probably wouldn't accomplish some of the things we want to do. Like you wouldn't have a job that you love and a chance to educate people about nature. I would never finish my dissertation and wouldn't pursue what interests me most."

"There's that to think about." They both sat in silence again. Emily sighed.

"I guess there's a balance in there somewhere."

"I think we'll find it, and we'll make life work, whatever comes. When you ended up alone in the woods at night with a concussion, you figured out how to survive and take care of yourself.'

"You figured out how to find me. When the drug dealers came to the cabin, you used your ability to run to save us all."

"You figured out how to drive like a race car driver in a movie chase scene."

Emily shivered. That had been a terrifying experience. It was exhilarating, though, when the car had turned around the way she expected.

"The research I've been doing about different times in history has so many examples of people who've gone through terrible times, but continued to live their lives. Even though it wasn't easy."

"So, we agree to live life to the fullest. And be careful." She paused. "Anyway, one thing I decided is to get rid of that chair Carl sat in. Every time I look at it, I think about him. It's just a used chair that I never liked much."

Ryan laughed. "Well, that's living on the edge, all right."

Emily pushed him and laughed. "Could you put it in the car tomorrow? My ankle feels pretty good, but I don't want to strain it. I'm going to take the chair to the Women's Resource Center resale place."

"Course. I'll put it in the car and take it there for you. Are you going to replace it?"

"Yes, I'm going to look at chairs and pick out something I really like."

Chapter 25

Sunday

Ryan's phone alarm went off, and he rolled out of bed, trying not to wake Emily. She woke while he was in the shower and got up to make coffee.

Ryan came into the kitchen and put his arms around her. "I know I've said this before. But I'm going to work on the dissertation all day today. No whining. No excuses. And I'm going to continue to do that until I'm finished. There are lots of things to explore in life, and you never know what might happen."

"Sounds like a good plan. I know you can do it."

"I'll get breakfast later. If I don't leave now, I could find lots of excuses to stick around. What are you going to do today?"

"Just get my life back in order. Do you want to go out tonight? We don't do that enough."

"Sounds good. I'll call you later, and we can decide where we'll go." Ryan kissed her, petted Carson, who was rubbing around his legs, and left.

Emily showered, dressed, and packed up her water bottle and snacks. She put her phone in her pocket and left a note on the table, saying where she was going. She left her camera behind and grabbed her jacket. She hadn't told Ryan she was going to hike the Loon Lake Trail and fill it with good memories. When she and Ryan had hiked it, she had felt afraid. The woods felt full of evil. Today she would clear those feelings away and think of the woods as friendly again.

Two cars were already at the trail, a Subaru Outback and a RAV4. No silver Ford SUV. She set out on the trail in the direction she had hiked before. An older couple was just coming off the trail. They smiled at her. "Great day for a hike."

"Yes, it's beautiful. Have a nice day."

'You, too."

Emily had decided that she would take her time and pay attention to her surroundings. She walked slowly, tried to notice everything around her, the trees, the flowers, birds singing. When she got to the seldom-used trail, she hesitated. She took a deep breath and enjoyed the caress of the breeze. She told herself there was nothing evil down this trail and turned down it.

She stopped at the large oak tree that Ryan had remembered and touched its bark. There were no tracks visible in the sand. A short while later, she spied the pine tree under which she had spent the night. She walked over and sat down beneath it. Patches of sun and shade dappled the woods, no dark threats to frighten her. She listened for the call of the owl, but didn't hear it. Still sleeping off its night prowl. She thought back to the red fox that had appeared suddenly, remembered her feelings of awe. What an exciting experience that was!

She stood up and walked back to the trail where she had encountered the bear. Closing her eyes, she recalled every detail of the bear and the feeling of connection when he had looked at her. Opening her eyes, she looked down the trail. In the distance she imagined she saw, a black bear ambling on its way into the woods, going somewhere safe, where he or she could continue just being a bear.

Acknowledgments

Although the trails cited in the novel are all based on real trails in Northern Michigan, trail names and details have been changed according to the needs of the story.

Many thanks to the following:

The naturalist class instructors at Northwestern Michigan College, who gave me the opportunity to learn more about the natural environment in Northern Michigan and to obtain a Naturalist Certificate.

The Grass River Natural Area's *Field Guide to Northwest Michigan: Its Flora, Fauna, Geology, and History* by James Dake, which helped me continue to identify flora and fauna in the area.

The Leelanau Conservancy, Grand Traverse Conservation District, and Sleeping Bear Dunes National Lakeshore, which preserve natural areas and provide trails for people to enjoy and learn from.

The many libraries in different cities that I have visited over the years, which gave me the opportunity to satisfy my love of books.

My first critique group of Mary Gallagher, Elsa, Sharon Blankenship, Lisa Patrol, and Claudia Boschitz, who encouraged me to share my writing.

Mark Bearman whose last name and interest in bears helped to inspire the story of rescuing the bear cub.

Melanie, Dom, and Reid Garzonio, who provided the inspiration for the character Reid, helped me to improve the novel as beta readers, and encouraged me with friendship and support. Welcome to Nico.

Ann Chalker, my mother, who encouraged my love of reading at an early age and shared an appreciation for nature. Char Brinkert, my sister, who wrote and illustrated "books" with me when we were children. And Edwin Chalker, my father, who valued education.

Briana Chalker, my daughter, who designed the cover for the book, provided insightful comments as a first reader, inspired the references to art, said,"You should publish this. Matt Girard, my son-in-law, who inspired the music and record collection references. And Morse, the athletic cat, who was the inspiration for Carson and is always an attentive host.

Peter Solenberger, my husband, who provided thoughtful comments, technical expertise, and continuous support throughout the process of writing and publishing.

www.ingramcontent.com/pod-product-compliance
Lightning Source LLC
Chambersburg PA
CBHW060452300726